P9-DKD-654

"So, I should sleep with you because..." Samantha teased

Nick smoothed his palms along her cheeks, weaving his fingers into her fragrant hair, tilting her gaze to meet his. "Because I'm offering you one night, just for us." He pressed his lips against her cheek. "One man." He kissed her chin, then placed a tender peck on the tip of her nose. "One woman." His hands trailed down her neck, dipping into the open collar of her robe. "One insatiable hunger."

Samantha's bold stare never left his. An expert negotiator, Nick appealed to what he knew she wanted most. "No strings, Sam. No expectations. Just one night of incredible pleasure."

Her gaze narrowed as she slipped her hands between them to work the knot on his robe. "You left out the most important detail, Nick."

She nuzzled close, grazing her lips over his bare chest. Instantly he knew what he'd forgotten. "Oh, you mean the part where I promise to make all your erotic fantasies come true?"

She stood so close, he could feel the thrill shimmy up her spine and light her eyes with hot fire.

"I didn't forget, Samantha. There are just some things that go without saying...."

Dear Reader,

Food—now, there's a topic I know and love. There's nothing more sensual than experimenting with new tastes and textures...okay, *almost* nothing. But combining my love for all things delicious with all things sexy seemed perfect for my first book in Temptation's new HEAT series!

When I finished writing *Pure Chance* (Temptation #814), I knew that Serena's sister, Samantha, was too irreverent, too sassy, too primed for a man to deny her a story of her own. Besides, I love New Orleans far too much to abandon the city after only one book. But Sam was a tough heroine to find a match for because she's so, well...tough.

Enter Dominick LaRocca. He's gorgeous. He's Italian. He's wealthy, powerful and trying hard as hell to achieve his goals. Poor man. Poor, poor man. Just when the last thing he needs is a beautiful, headstrong woman, Samantha practically pushes her way into his life and turns his careful plans upside down.

Sound like fun? I think so. Please let me know if you agree. You can drop me a line at P.O. Box 270885, Tampa, FL 33688-0885, or visit my Web site at www.julieleto.com.

Salute!

Julie Elizabeth Leto

P.S. Be sure to watch for my first book in Harlequin's newest—and hottest—series yet: Blaze! *Exposed,* the first book in the SEXY CITY NIGHTS miniseries, will heat up the bookstores in August 2001. Don't miss it!

INSATIABLE
Julie Elizabeth Leto

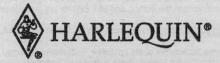

HARLEQUIN®

TORONTO • NEW YORK • LONDON
AMSTERDAM • PARIS • SYDNEY • HAMBURG
STOCKHOLM • ATHENS • TOKYO • MILAN • MADRID
PRAGUE • WARSAW • BUDAPEST • AUCKLAND

If you purchased this book without a cover you should be aware
that this book is stolen property. It was reported as "unsold and
destroyed" to the publisher, and neither the author nor the
publisher has received any payment for this "stripped book."

For my wonderful aunts—Rose, Fae and Anita,
women I admire and love with all my heart.
I count myself incredibly lucky to have been
born into a family that includes you.

And for "Nana" Caroline LaRocca and "Nanie" Velia Leto.
You showed us all what love and family loyalty
are all about. I miss you both.

ISBN 0-373-25935-2

INSATIABLE

Copyright © 2001 by Julie Leto Klapka.

All rights reserved. Except for use in any review, the reproduction or
utilization of this work in whole or in part in any form by any electronic,
mechanical or other means, now known or hereafter invented, including
xerography, photocopying and recording, or in any information storage
or retrieval system, is forbidden without the written permission of the
publisher, Harlequin Enterprises Limited, 225 Duncan Mill Road,
Don Mills, Ontario, Canada M3B 3K9.

All characters in this book have no existence outside the imagination of
the author and have no relation whatsoever to anyone bearing the same
name or names. They are not even distantly inspired by any individual
known or unknown to the author, and all incidents are pure invention.

This edition published by arrangement with Harlequin Books S.A.

® and TM are trademarks of the publisher. Trademarks indicated with
® are registered in the United States Patent and Trademark Office, the
Canadian Trade Marks Office and in other countries.

Visit us at www.eHarlequin.com

Printed in U.S.A.

1

"COULDN'T YOU just eat him up?"

If Samantha Deveaux heard the question one more time this morning, she was going to puke. After two weeks on the job at Louisiana Superdome security, her assignment at the SuperMarketing Expo was testing her mettle most. Last week's Wrestlemania had been a cakewalk next to this. At least there she'd known what to expect. Screaming. Cursing. A tussle or two. Just enough unpredictable rowdiness to keep her busy.

But since the Supermarketing Expo's eight o'clock opening, she'd gone from rolling her eyes to groaning aloud at the increasingly bad puns. In four hours, every female in the Dome, and a few men for that matter, had strolled through the wide section of wall-less, corporate-sponsored booths and eventually stopped to make a comment in front of the display by LaRocca Foods. Their snickers and sly remarks relied on a combination of food imagery and naughty sexual innuendo.

All for the man looming across from her position at the end of the aisle. Not in person, fortunately, but on a gargantuan aluminum and enamel replica of LaRocca Food's best-selling pasta sauce in a jar—the centerpiece of their display—complete with a huge label stretched across the middle.

In the label's center, a bare-chested man, sketched with lifelike precision, glistened with sweat as he toiled in the middle of some Mediterranean olive field. He had all the classic features of a Sicilian supermodel: ebony hair worn long and windblown, eyes tinted the color of green Italian marble, and a chest, arms and legs that would put Michelangelo's *David* to shame.

He's hotter than his marinara sauce.

He can toss my pasta anytime.

And then the succinct, but equally charged, *Mmm, mmm, good.*

Samantha had seen his type many times before, but even her jaded attitude didn't deter her gaze from roaming back to that label.

His eyes drew her. Not just because of their Kodachrome color, but because an elusive, alluring emotion charged his emerald gaze with power, intensity. The man had attitude. Presence. Even in still life, he demanded attention.

His grin, sly enough to be sultry and subtle enough to make her wonder what he was *really* thinking, said, "Eat this, I dare you. And if you do, I'll give you an equally delicious reward."

As if the man on the label had leaned down from his rustic field and murmured his challenge only to Samantha, a spark of awareness flared as a fantasy formed in her mind. A wicked tryst. A delicious dalliance. Her thighs clenched, instinctively attempting to sate the hot tickle deep inside her, an all-too-frequent reminder that she hadn't had a man in her life for *way* too long. She closed her eyes for an instant, battling to block the flash of flesh and folly that haunted her lately. Day and night. Asleep or awake.

Unfortunately, her once-indistinct fantasy lover now had a face and a body—a face and a body she obviously couldn't resist. She closed her eyes to block his image, reminding herself that he was nothing more than the artistic rendering of some obviously anatomically obsessed artist, but the sensual stream of heat continued its course upward, quivering in her belly then tightening her breasts. Her self-imposed celibacy, enforced for almost a year, had taken its toll. Sam pressed her lips together and fought the sensations— determined to stay focused. Success would be a valiant feat for a girl who'd discovered her sexuality way too early and only recently recognized that her wild past had actually been a blind search for love and acceptance.

And a few sinful dreams were tolerable as long as she managed to put herself back on track. With her attention on the neon-lit soda logo directly across from her, she began silently reciting the techniques she'd learned in her Internet course on how to disarm a crazed stalker.

Despite the repetition, the unspoken invitation from the man in the olive field still echoed loud and clear.

"So, it's the new girl who rates the choice spot. Enjoying the view, Deveaux?"

Samantha's attention snapped to her left and connected with Ruby Gumbert's wry smile. The retired cop, barely ten years older than Samantha, viewed the world with a laid-back cynicism that Samantha couldn't help admiring. They'd become fast friends, though Sam would never admit just how choice she considered her vantage point across from LaRocca Foods to be. She didn't have to. The minute Ruby slid her *Terminator*-style sunglasses down her nose, she let out the most impressive catcall whistle Sam had ever heard from a woman.

"Who'd you sleep with to get this assignment?" Ruby asked.

"Who'd I sleep with?" Samantha counted back six months to her move from Hollywood, California, to her return to New Orleans. After adding another six months to account for brooding after her breakup with Anthony, Sam shook her head. No wonder the Pasta God had her on the sexual edge of insanity. In this entire year, she hadn't slept with anyone but her older sister's cat, Tabitha II. Unless she counted Maurice. Which she didn't. He was Serena's mixed-breed sheepdog, and unlike her Himalayan feline, he preferred the cool floor to the cozy bed.

"I figured I must have insulted someone," Sam quipped. "Listening to all the *oohs* and *ahs* isn't exactly my idea of an ideal workday." *Neither is swallowing my own oohs and ahs, thank you very much.*

Samantha forced her gaze away from the damn label that inspired all the appreciative groans. Some women were such suckers for a pretty face. Even she had been once, dating some of Hollywood's heartthrobs, even living with Anthony Marks, the biggest cardiac arrester of them all. Thanks to her father, famed action-flick director Devlin Deveaux, she'd met and mingled with every male celebrity ever chosen as *People* magazine's Sexiest Man Alive, and more future coverboys than she cared to count.

And yet, this Pasta God had her fantasizing about new and interesting uses for extra virgin olive oil just from a pencil-drawn ad.

"If you want a lesson in bad pick-up lines," Sam concluded, "you should trade places with me." Sam watched another gaggle of suited, female conventioneers leer and snicker as they strolled by the sexy label. "If you want excitement and mayhem, unfortunately, this isn't the place."

Ruby's smile curled with ageless wisdom. "Life ain't like the movies, Deveaux. Mostly, this job is standing around, looking tough and politely asking people to follow the rules. Not to mention giving directions to the bathroom."

Samantha stepped down from the box dais that provided a clear vantage of her area and wished she hadn't made such a disparaging remark. She already strongly suspected that once again, this job wasn't going to work out. She'd tried approximately four other professions in the past six months and nothing kept her interest. Except for becoming a personal bodyguard. That one really had her blood pumping. If only her brother-in-law, bodyguard Brandon Chance, would come home from his honeymoon with her sister so they could get to work. He'd already put her on the payroll, but with Brandon out of the country and no clients to serve, Sam had done little but earn some of her certifications and licenses and spend the petty cash on neat gadgets. She'd taken the security job at the Dome for two reasons—to pay back the money Brandon had originally budgeted for office rent and electricity and, at Brandon's suggestion, to garner some experience.

So far, all she'd learned was that her attention span was shorter than even her second-grade tutor would have imagined. Oh, and that she could now be aroused by a pencil-drawn hottie on a pasta-jar label.

"I don't mean to insult the job, Ruby. I know you love it. It's just..."

Ruby pushed the sunglasses higher on the bridge of her nose. "Not what you expected. Never is, 'specially with your background. Pretty girl like you. Working in the movies, living the good life..."

"Define *good*," Samantha interrupted, well aware that Ruby was teasing. They'd had this conversation over coffee at Café du Monde after last week's Julio Iglesias concert. During her Hollywood childhood, Sam had always had food in her belly and a roof over her head—if take-out Chinese and trailers on movie lots counted. Her father had loved her in the way only a self-absorbed genius could, meaning that he showered her with affection whenever he didn't have something more important to do.

A child thrust into an adult world from the age of five, Samantha was lucky to have escaped relatively unscathed—at least on the surface. She was only now starting to repair the damage to her heart. Her life in Hollywood could not be described as *good* unless the standards were incredibly shallow.

Ruby's chuckle lacked humor. "*Good* always is a relative term. For today, *this* is a good job. No worries. Easy money. Who knows what tomorrow will bring?"

Samantha frowned, knowing full well what she'd encounter tomorrow—another day of watching conventioneers stuff food samples into their mouths while planning to cut out early and hit the bars on Bourbon Street. Samantha had wished this temporary job would work out, but she had her heart set on a career whose main benefit would be excitement. A little danger. Maybe she'd be lucky and there'd be a scuffle over the free tortilla chips or a grab for the Godiva. Anything to keep her from hijacking the next flight to Brazil so she could drag her brother-in-law back to the States.

"You sound like my mother," Samantha said. "Sometimes I think she forgets that she stole 'Tomorrow is another day' from Scarlett. Unfortunately, I've always been a *now* and *today* kind of person. You're less disappointed by life that way."

"Are you? Less disappointed?" Ruby shook her head and grinned, her bob of raven hair not daring to move from where she'd gelled the strands in place. "Just wait until Signore Gorgeous makes his appearance. That ought to liven things up."

Samantha swallowed her shock.

"The LaRocca model is coming here?"

"That's the scoop. They'd be stupid to keep him under wraps. He's the hottest draw I've seen in the Superdome since Mike Ditka coached the Saints." Ruby lowered her shades. "Whoever he is, the man's a god."

Samantha felt inordinately annoyed she couldn't argue that point without sounding like a big fat liar. Gorgeous men, real or in pictures, simply weren't on her agenda anymore. She was done equating lust with love—with allowing her passions to triumph over cool thinking and common sense. She'd banked on coming home to Louisiana to find her focus. But since her job experience consisted of baby-sitting her father—a creative prodigy who could barely balance his checkbook—and stunt work that kept Devlin's high-priced actors out of harm's way, Sam wasn't exactly a good candidate for the secretarial pool.

Her life had always been about adventure. Thrills. Discovery. When Devlin left her mother and sister in New Orleans after the divorce, Sam had followed, anxious even at five to see the world with her father, to live on location and mingle with the stars. She'd even appeared in a few films until she hit those awkward teenage years. By then, Sam had already begun to despise the celebrity spotlight. Becoming a stunt double had been the perfect profession—anonymous but exciting.

Then she'd been injured. She'd moved in with Anthony, followed a few months later by their heart-wrenching breakup. Returning to New Orleans after twenty-three years hadn't been easy, but she'd come determined to heal all her wounds—physical and emotional—start over and reconnect with her family.

She'd made some headway. Her agility and strength were at one hundred percent. She no longer thought about Anthony every day or about the choices she *should* have made. The future beckoned.

Unfortunately, even romantic, outrageous New Orleans had held little promise by way of truly exciting career choices, until her sister married Brandon. Too bad the eldest Chance brother, in addition to his military background, had an insatiable sexual appetite that kept the couple on their honeymoon four weeks past their scheduled return date. Or maybe Sam should blame her sister. Surrendering to passion seemed to be a genetic trait.

Aw, hell. She couldn't blame either of them. She'd never been one to deny her own desires—and she'd never even really been in love. Sam couldn't begrudge her sister or Brandon their wedded bliss, but she still wished they'd be blissful at home.

In the meantime, Brandon had suggested that Sam pull some security gigs for hands-on learning. Nothing too risky, he'd insisted. Her stunt-work training gave her physical agility and mental preparedness, but the movie sets, speeding cars and fireball explosions had been controlled. Carefully planned and painfully executed. She needed to experience the unexpected—learn to trust her gut.

Somehow, she doubted the Supermarketing Expo fit the bill.

"Samantha, this is Mitchell. Respond please."

Samantha unhooked the walkie-talkie from her belt and turned from the chatter and music echoing through the professionally designed booths and displays. "Deveaux, here."

"The CEO of LaRocca Foods is on his way to his booth. He's a major player. Tim's with him. Stand tall."

Samantha smirked. Another executive type headed toward his company's booth and another opportunity for the security staff to play Secret Service to people whose importance hardly warranted professional protection. Except for the guys at the front assigned to allow entrance to paid conventioneers, the Expo was hardly high-risk. Now, if Mr. Model-licious did indeed plan an appearance as rumored, Sam might get her wish. Mass hysteria and raging female hormones could cause a very dangerous mix.

She knew that firsthand.

"Gotcha, boss."

"And tell Gumbert to return to her position."

Ruby slipped her glasses back onto her regal nose. "I guess the ogle-fest is over. Back to ice-cream land. How the heck do they expect me to stay on this diet when they keep handing me samples of mint chocolate chip? Still want to trade?"

Samantha shook her head. She had few weaknesses in the world, but one was definitely butter pecan ice cream, which she knew they were also serving at the booth near Ruby's station.

"Fat chance."

Ruby patted her flat tummy. "Fat is right. Have fun with the big shot."

Samantha saluted then snapped the walkie-talkie back onto her belt, slipped her hands behind her back and waited for the corporate executive to rush by and ignore her diligence. She hated this job. She hated hating this job. So far, the only good thing to come of her move was being closer to her sister and mother—and again, the definition of *good* came into question.

Her sister, when not honeymooning in some South American country, was a trip in herself—and gave new meaning to the term *unconventional*. Her mother, a world-renowned medium and self-proclaimed New Orleans spirit guide, defied any and all definitions. But so far, Endora had been supportive of Samantha's return, even when she'd taken this "rent-a-cop" deal to supplement her income instead of accepting Mommy's proffered handout.

Which she wouldn't need if her father hadn't reinvested the money he owed her from her last job into his upcoming film. He'd named her as a producer and assumed she'd be thrilled. She could end up obscenely rich if the movie proved a hit. Too bad Sam didn't care about vulgar wealth. She just wanted to be comfortable, stable and self-sufficient. A couple of months under her brother-in-law's tutelage and she'd be a fully licensed, salary-earning bodyguard. She'd already obtained her concealed-weapon permit and had begun her coursework over the Internet. Now she needed some on-the-job training.

But four weeks after their first scheduled return date, Brandon and Serena were still sunning and loving on a beach in Rio de Janeiro. Never mind that Sam had bought and installed a state-of-the-art computer system. Never mind that she'd used next month's office rent to invest in several tracking devices, night-vision goggles and the smallest communications mechanisms she'd ever seen. They'd be the best-outfitted outfit in the personal-protection game.

If they didn't go out of business first. Okay, that was an overstatement. She'd only spent a couple thousand of the petty cash and next month's office rent. But if she didn't restore the treasury soon, she'd have to call Brandon and ask for more money—and admit she'd spent *slightly* more than he'd authorized.

A growing disturbance near the west entrance caught her eye, sending her senses to alert mode. Flanked by two security guards, a threesome of somber-faced suits made their way through the crowd. Sam recognized the first man as Tim Tousignant, the dynamic young executive at the helm of the massive Expo and the man who'd approved her assignment. Good-looking and driven, he impressed Sam with his desire to run any event with smooth precision. Not enough to accept his invitation to dinner, but Sam didn't mix business with pleasure. Not anymore.

The woman on his left, a tall, dark beauty with luminous olive skin clutched a stack of presentation folders and barely contained a wry smile as she glanced at the growing crowd. She leaned nearer to the man in the center and said something she obviously thought was hilarious.

Nearly a head taller than the others, the CEO of LaRocca Foods obviously didn't agree. He shot his companion a sharp look and muttered a few words that caused her laughter to die a quick death. He watched his feet and held his hand up to the growing number of followers in a gesture more like a "stop" sign than a wave.

Samantha's skin prickled.

Lured by the presence of this reluctant Pied Piper, people left the other displays to follow the hulking executive and his burgeoning entourage toward Sam's end of the aisle near the north exit. An electric buzz rippled through the Superdome until waves of convention goers, mostly female, rushed toward the five-hundred-square-foot area reserved by LaRocca Foods. Mitchell said the CEO, right? She glanced at the label again, then back at the man in the middle of the swarming horde.

Her heart skittered, but then she smiled. A few moments ago, the man's incredible looks and intense gaze, captured on the pasta label, had affected her like a virulent potion. Now she had the perfect antidote—his obvious arrogance.

If he wasn't the end-all, be-all of shameless self-promotion, she didn't know who was. Mr. Chief Executive Officer, sans the top half of his pressed Italian suit, was indeed the sexy hunk-o-rama on his newest product.

Samantha started to laugh, but stopped when the security guards approached, their eyes wide as the swollen throng closed in. A few women squealed. Manicured hands reached across the guards, grabbing at the CEO who still walked, head down, until the mob stopped his progress.

"Oh, God, it's him! Dominick LaRocca!" someone shrieked.

"You can dig in my field anytime, Pasta Man!"

"I'm hungry for more than sauce, hot stuff! Over here!"

For an instant, Sam thought she'd been transported onto Bourbon Street during Mardi Gras. A middle-aged woman in a silk blouse lifted her shirt and bra to the delight of every man within leering distance. The crowd, effectively incited, surged, pressing the small group of five to the wall. Sam jumped onto the dais to regain her fix on LaRocca and company.

Time to work.

She radioed for backup, then shouted at the two security guards ineffectively trying to hold the women back with drawn nightsticks. Folders scattered as the pretty olive-skinned woman twisted in front of her boss to put one more barrier between him and the tentacles of hungry hands. Sam lost sight of Tim altogether, but figured protecting the man at the center of the disturbance was priority one, especially since he was the one *causing* the melee.

She couldn't wait for the guards to lead him closer to the exit. She tucked her hair under her cap and slipped into the crowd, diving low and pushing through the writhing mass until she reached her colleagues. They begged the women to stand aside, using minimal force despite the growing danger.

"I called for backup," Samantha yelled before pressing between the ineffective wall they'd formed to keep the CEO from harm. "Keep them back!"

"One heck of a security plan you have here," La-Rocca growled.

She ignored him and grabbed his elbow.

"Follow me."

"Wait. Where's Anita?"

Samantha felt certain Anita would fare better once the object of these women's desires was removed from the hall.

"She'll be fine once you're safe."

"Wait!"

Undoubtedly used to calling the shots, he dodged her attempts to pull him out. Samantha knew better than to argue, especially when only about every third word could be heard over the fervent screaming, blatant offers of sex and even a marriage proposal or two, if you counted "marry me, marry me!" as a true invitation. Instead, Sam twisted around him and used her full body weight to shove him to the exit. The sheer velocity of her push sent the crowd fumbling and tripping over one another, allowing her the split second she needed to squeeze him through the heavy security door.

She slipped in behind him and immediately threw her back against the door to attempt to close and lock it.

"Which one are you, anyway?" she asked, annoyed. "George, John, Paul or Ringo?"

A growl tore from her throat as she met with resistance from the other side.

Sex-crazed bimbos! Desperate, man-stupid teenyboppers!

"Don't be shy," LaRocca said between pants. "Tell them what you really think."

She'd tossed him into the hallway so forcefully, he'd hit the opposite wall with a grunt. The loosened knot in his tie had flipped over his collar and the left hip pocket of his jacket hung loose at his side. His nostrils flared as he gasped for breath, then he used the opposite wall to launch himself against the door.

Against her.

The contact cracked the air around them with a pop nearly inaudible with women screaming on the other side of the door. But the surge of static electricity burned Samantha from the outer layer of her skin straight through to her heart. She shook her head, trying to dispel the resonating tingle, and pressed her back to the door. She dug in with her powerful legs, legs now tangled between the Pasta God's marble thighs. His scent was as crisp and clean as his starched white shirt, as if he'd just stepped out of the shower.

The image of him in nothing but a fluffy white towel immediately sprang to mind.

"Did I say that out loud?" she asked, hoping like hell that he'd interpret the flush of her skin as natural exertion, even embarrassment at her mouthy tirade. She refused to look up in his face, though gazing straight into his chest wasn't any less dangerous when she knew, thanks to the sauce label, exactly what his chest looked like bare.

"Loud and clear. But I'm not arguing. You'd think these women had never seen a man before." He struggled to help her close the door, but hands and fingers, even an ankle or two stuck through the six inches of space between the steel barrier and quiet freedom. Over the noise from the other side, Sam finally heard the arrival of reinforcements.

"Back. Back. Move back!"

Hands and feet disappeared from the doorway, but the press from the other side remained constant, probably from the guards struggling to clear the doorway. They wouldn't be safe until they closed the door, and her counterparts on the other side apparently had their hands full just blocking the exit.

Glancing down at her for approval, Dominick La-Rocca took another deep breath. "On three."

She nodded, bracing herself for further impact. The rush of adrenaline snapped her head up. *Good Lord. He's going to throw his weight against the door. Against me!*

He counted, "One..."

His eyes mirrored the color of freshly crushed mint. "Two..."

His jaw looked chiseled from flesh-toned granite.

"Three!"

Pressed Italian silk didn't hide an erection worth a damn.

2

NICK THREW HIS FULL weight into shutting the door. In his mad rush, he trapped the sapphire-eyed security guard beneath him. The latch caught and a sensation not unlike an electric shock snapped all around him. Instantaneous stimulation surged through his blood and rushed straight to his groin.

He hadn't expected the spitfire in uniform to have anything soft about her, anything luscious or feminine. He'd been wrong. Just the brief contact stirred the primal male urge he'd kept in careful check for so long— a self-restraint made especially difficult with women of various degrees of desirability making offers any sane man couldn't refuse. Yet, as she pushed the deadbolt into place, the lush warmth of her curves hugged him straight through his jacket, shirt and tie, making him wish he could forget his responsibilities to his family. Just this once.

"Sorry." He rolled aside, straightening his suit, trying to ignore that his skin tingled as if he'd just been struck by lightning. His grandmothers often mused that a thunderbolt would probably strike him dead before he met a woman who could stir him out of his rigid, business-and-family-first way of thinking.

For once, Rosalia LaRocca and Rafaela Durante might be wrong.

"I'm the one who should apologize." Her eyes reflected blue like the sun-sparkling water of a swimming pool. On a scorching day. One hundred and ten degrees. In the shade. But before he drowned in her liquid irises, she turned aside, patting her slim waist as she checked the presence of her nightstick, walkie-talkie and keys. The moisture in Nick's mouth evaporated.

"The Expo isn't really prepared for mass hysteria," she added, chastisement totally undisguised. "Don't you have personal security?"

Her snippy tone reminded him of the reasons *why* he'd been without a lover for so long—why his body was primed for sexual games he couldn't afford to play. Ever since his picture made it onto that label, women he'd never met had been offering to do things for him—to him—that even his ex-fiancée would consider depraved. He'd received naked snapshots in the mail, wrapped in lacy panties that had obviously been worn. Just last night, a woman in a bikini had ambushed them at the airport, throwing herself spread-eagle over the hood of his hired limousine.

His family had been hounding him to employ a bodyguard, but the last thing he needed was some goon in a dark suit following him around as if he were John Gotti or Al Capone. No thanks. He had enough trouble with Italian stereotypes without traveling with hired muscle.

"I'm a businessman, not a celebrity."

"Care to tell that to the women on the other side of this door?" She turned and moved to undo the lock.

"No." He rushed to grab her hand, stopping short

when she smiled, winked and released the latch. He smoothed his palm over his hair, attempting a nonchalant recovery. Too bad there was nothing nonchalant about the wave of disappointment that rolled over him because he couldn't touch her again. Ever.

Man, he had to put a stop to this hysteria soon. The barrage of willing women, coupled with his decision to neglect his personal life and personal needs, at least until the European distribution deal solidified LaRocca Food's solvency, threatened to undo him.

And the adorable pucker on the security guard's lips wasn't helping one damn bit.

"*That* mob shouldn't have happened," he insisted, jabbing his finger at the door in an attempt to regain his trademark snarl.

She shrugged. "Shouldn't have is one thing, but it did. What did you expect anyway? Your picture on that label is more provocative than most *Playgirl* centerfolds."

Nick jammed his hand through his hair again, reminding himself that this woman's haughtiness and her all-too-true observation were insufficient reasons to lose his temper. The label *was* provocative. He had the sales figures to prove it.

"That picture was not my doing."

She crossed her arms and shifted her weight to one leg. The pose was disbelief and sassiness potently combined. "You are the CEO of that company, aren't you?"

"CEO, but not chairman. Some decisions can be made without my knowledge. Or at least, they could *before*."

"This isn't just a little bit about your ego? All those women screaming? Tearing at your clothes?"

His eyebrows shot up. He wasn't used to talking turkey with a stranger. "You don't mince words, do you?" he asked.

"No point. I'm a call-'em-like-I-see-'em kind of gal."

And he usually didn't find that trait desirable.

Usually.

"Well, you're seeing this one all wrong."

His grandmothers, the joint chairwomen of the La-Rocca board of directors, had schemed with marketing and production to come up with the new label with his picture on it, enhanced to make him some sort of romantic hero. Before he could fire the artist, sales skyrocketed. All the traditional leaders in the sauce business were still scrambling to catch up.

In the midst of a marketing coup, Nick had hoped this trip to New Orleans would allow him to recapture his once iron-hand grip on his personal life. But not only had his grandmothers seen fit to put his image on the label, they'd included some rather clever copy lamenting his single marital status and celebrating his estimated net worth.

He hadn't known so many single women lived in the United States. Women in every demographic group had flooded the mailroom with offers of marriage. Eager brides congregated in the lobby of his headquarters on Chicago's Walker Drive. It was only a matter of time before they set up camp at his Lake Shore condominium.

He'd come to New Orleans eager for a little peace and quiet, not to mention anonymity. The last thing he needed was another headstrong female in his life, even if she had just saved his hide from the desperate throng.

"I'm featured in that booth because ever since that damn label was introduced, *without my knowledge*," he added a second time, "sales have gone up forty-seven percent in the past two weeks alone."

"Ah, the bottom line," she said with a nod. "I can understand that."

Great. Another woman with dollar signs in her eyes. Wonderful. Too bad that insight didn't diminish his growing fascination with the gently bowed, slightly glossy shape and texture of her lips.

"Is there a way out of here?" he demanded. "A private way?"

The security guard looked around to catch her bearings. He noticed that the gold tag on her shirt read "Deveaux."

"Are you staying at the Hyatt next door?" she asked.

"Yes."

"Then follow me. There's a lower tunnel reserved for authorized personnel. It'll lead you out the back and all we'll have to do is cross a parking lot."

She swept her hand forward then started toward a stairwell that would take them to ground level. Her step was light and trouble-free, saucy and sexy and dangerous as hell. Her hips rocked with a rhythm only she could hear—but Nick tuned in, despite his best efforts not to. Queen during their hey-day. Joan Jett and Pat Benatar jamming with the Bangles.

He moistened his lips, wondering if he'd ever met a

woman who could make him regret so much and want so much, so fast.

"Thank you for taking control out there," he said, knowing he owed her some genuine gratitude and hoping a little more conversation would tamp down his growing physical interest. He reminded himself that she had a sharp tongue and decisive opinions—two strikes for any woman he wasn't related to by blood. As much as he'd tried, he couldn't change the LaRocca women or their daughters. And as much as he loved them, he didn't need another headstrong woman trying to lead him by the nose.

"The guards assigned to me didn't seem to know what to do," he added.

"Yeah, well, they're guys," she concluded quickly. "They probably figured too much force and they'd hurt someone."

Nick chuckled. "I don't doubt that you could do some serious damage if you wanted to."

"Considering my height and weight, it takes a concerted effort for me to hurt someone." She spoke brusquely, totally oblivious to the double meaning to his comment.

Or at least, he assumed she was oblivious. He wasn't so sure when he caught her sharp glance and a fleeting grin. "Women in my field compensate with speed, agility and, well...brains."

Not to mention soft curves, dark blond hair and bright blue eyes. The woman who'd saved him, he decided, was as close to lethal as strychnine.

"Have you been a security guard long?" Nick knew he shouldn't have asked the question, shouldn't have invited more conversation. The more she talked, the more he wanted to know.

"About two weeks," she said, her voice softening as she admitted her inexperience. He never would have guessed she was a rookie. His fascination with her jumped a notch. "But this is just a temporary job. Until my boss gets back from his honeymoon." She paused, biting her bottom lip before admitting, "I'm a protection specialist with No Chances Protection." Her claim grew louder as she spoke, as if she was trying the label on for size.

"Protection specialist?" he asked.

"A bodyguard."

After his brush with the screaming crowd, Nick couldn't begrudge his savior her choice of occupation. In fact, he was having a damn hard time begrudging anything at the moment. Just walking behind her, watching the alluring swing of her hips, catching the light in those impressive blue eyes whenever she looked over her shoulder, did amazing things to his outlook. His cousin and assistant, Anita, had started calling him the ogre at least ten times a day. Right now, he felt like the prince who slew the ogre...all for the sake of a sexy blond princess.

And he didn't appreciate the feeling one iota.

Everything about Miss Deveaux should have gone against his grain. She was tough. She spoke her mind. She took control and did what had to be done without regrets.

A fine combination for a lover, ordinarily, but a horrible mix when he couldn't afford to extend an invitation to his bed unless it was attached to a marriage proposal. And though Miss Deveaux stirred his blood like a chef with a swift wooden spoon, this woman's medley of sassy confidence was the last thing he wanted to deal with for a lifetime.

Nick knew his preferences for a bride—sweet, submissive, maybe a little shy—were about a century behind the times, but he'd yet to meet someone who inspired him to change.

And though he was the last heterosexual man on earth who *wanted* to get married, he couldn't deny that very, very soon, he'd have little to no choice.

When his grandmothers decided last year that they wouldn't retire and turn the company completely over to him until he settled down and started a family, he should have popped the question to the nearest single adult female and been done with it. Instead, he'd dug in his heels and refused to let them dictate his private life.

Only, his private life consisted of endless family obligations—weddings, baptisms, birthdays—an occasional jog down Lake Shore and, perhaps, a night out with his CFO and vice president of retail sales so they could discuss business under the guise of relaxation.

Their latest discussion was the conundrum his grandmothers had created with their declaration. If Rose and Fae died before he married, LaRocca Foods would be sold in pieces to various family members. The conglomerate he'd worked so hard to build would cease to exist. All the market power he'd amassed since he joined the company just out of college would be lost.

The LaRoccas and Durantes had never been wealthy before. Until he took over the business, they had strug-

gled through two generations of barely making ends
meet, of not sending children to college if they couldn't
win scholarships, of doubling up on living arrangements to make sure every mouth was fed. But when
the family's restaurant fell on hard times and his
grandmothers started supplementing the family income by selling their pasta sauce from behind the register, it had been Nick's idea to build a display case for
the West Monroe Street entrance. He'd been the one to
organize and offer mail order to tourists and, after
completing his course of study at the University of Il-
linois, he'd personally pounded the pavement to introduce their products to grocery stores. And just seven
years ago, he'd spearheaded the promotion campaign
that pushed their private stock into the public marketplace for a premium price.

And all without putting his own picture on a single
label.

Nick quickened his step to match Miss Deveaux's
momentum. "I can make it to my room alone, thank
you. Just tell me which door leads to the stairwell."

She shook her head, a few more strands of blond
spilling out to brush her shoulders. "That's not the way
we do things in Louisiana," she said proudly, adding a
Creole lilt to her accent-free voice. "This is a Southern
state, remember? Hospitality and all that."

"Yes, well, I'm from Chicago. We do things just fine
on our own. The last thing I need is another woman
clamoring to hold my hand."

She stopped her progression down the hall and impaled him with a look of utter disbelief. "I've met lots
of people from Chicago and not one was downright

rude. Excuse me for pointing out the obvious, but I did just save your hide. And I didn't touch your hands in the process."

He didn't want to think about what she *had* touched. And how that touching had sent his pulse rate skyrocketing.

"You have my gratitude." He reached for his wallet, but the widening of her azure eyes to the size of jar lids stopped him from offering money for her service. He pocketed his eelskin billfold. "If you could just point me to the right door?"

The sassy security guard with the name Deveaux stitched above her left breast—a rather pert, curvaceous breast—slid her cap off her head, releasing the full, bouncy tumble of her hair. She eyed him head to toe, a growing distaste skewing her bowed lips into an unattractive sneer.

"The blue door at the end of the hall."

He nodded to her curtly—just to make sure she didn't follow him—and proceeded in the direction she'd indicated. Insulting women hadn't been a mainstay of his behavior until recently, when Nana Rose and Nana Fae schemed to make him the most eligible bachelor on the Fortune 500. With the gleeful help of his cousin, Anita, they'd successfully transformed him from a driven businessman into a cynical, overbearing slave driver. He had no right to take his frustration out on Miss Deveaux, but she had the unfortunate luck to be the nearest woman in range of his anger. He'd dictate a letter of commendation to her superiors as soon as he found Anita.

Yanking at the latch on the door she'd indicated, he

turned his thoughts from the woman behind him to plotting how he could reschedule his appearance at the booth. He'd planned to glad-hand some of the industry's largest chains into awarding his products more shelf space and additional end-cap promotions. He'd be damned if he'd abandon his short-term goals for the Expo just because his grandmothers intended to make him the Fabio of the grocery business.

As he walked across the threshold, a distinctly feminine squeal snapped up his head.

"It's him! Marry me, Pasta Man!"

Nick glanced over his shoulder at the slowly closing blue door. She'd said "blue," right? Yet he was now standing in the registration area of the Expo instead of a stairwell to his hotel. And one by one, recognition dawned on the faces of several women just a few feet away.

Here I go again.

SERVES HIM RIGHT.

From behind, Samantha watched LaRocca's fists clench. His shoulders tightened. She could only imagine the look on his face—and the horror she pictured gave an extra curve to the smile bowing her mouth. Some men had to learn the hard way. Samantha Deveaux was not a woman to be dismissed. Someone might do it once. But twice? Not likely. Not anymore.

Disheveled and distraught, the women being escorted out of the Superdome struggled against the careful grasps of several annoyed security guards. As Sam figured, her co-workers had reached the main lobby to escort the rowdiest women out of the Expo

Hall to cool off. She'd just stoked the flame by misleading the lion right back into the den.

She considered letting the blue door slam shut behind Dominick LaRocca, leaving him at the mercy of the hormonally charged females on the other side, but her duty to protect him intruded on her fun. Pushing the door open at the last possible minute, she allowed him to slip back into the hall before the crowd attacked again.

"Did I say *blue?*" she asked once the door slammed shut, sugar dripping from each syllable. "I meant gold. The gold door is the stairwell, the blue door leads to the lobby." She pointed to each as she spoke, as if willing herself to remember facts she obviously knew perfectly well.

A storm swirled in his eyes, reminding her of a deadly waterspout in the gulf. "That was uncalled for," he snapped, once again trying to straighten his tie and jacket despite that he looked as if he'd just...well, as if he'd just escaped a screaming crowd of crazed women clamoring for his bod.

"I beg to differ." Samantha planted her fists on her hips. "I'd say it was completely called for. You were rude and I *won't* be treated like a groupie. My job—in addition to saving your butt—is to escort you to safety. If you won't let me do that job, then I can't be responsible for the consequences."

He stood straighter as he caught his breath, and Samantha suddenly found his height imposing. If it weren't for the twinkle of amusement dancing in his green eyes, she might have backed down. "So you led me back into the ring? Revenge, quick and simple. That's a concept I understand."

She shook her head. "I don't believe in revenge." Samantha considered that claim for a minute and decided it wasn't entirely truthful. It had been. Once. When she didn't know better. "No, that's not true. I do believe in revenge. In fact, I kind of dig it."

"*Dig it?* How old are you?"

"Old enough to have a father who still says 'dig it' and 'groovy.' And for the record, it isn't considered polite to ask a woman her age."

"Well, aren't you just New Orleans' answer to Miss Manners. I suppose it's the height of proper etiquette to throw a drowning man back into shark-infested waters?" He gestured toward the blue door, his expression incredulous.

She pursed her lips. "We could call it even."

Despite his best efforts, a tiny grin broke through his scowl. "Very reasonable. Now, if you'd be so kind, Miss Deveaux, would you personally escort me to some quiet exit so I can return to my hotel?"

"Name's Samantha. And I'd be delighted to see you safely out of the Dome, Mr. LaRocca."

He hesitated, then thrust his hand forward in a businesslike pose. "Nick. Please."

Sam glanced at his eyes first, then his hand, assessing the threat of touching him. The feel of him against her still resonated throughout the full length of her body, still lingered along the edges of her skin. But her newfound independence and determination wouldn't allow her to refuse.

She concentrated all of her strength into giving him

one hearty handshake, but was ill prepared for the electric shock that crackled between their palms.

"Ow!"

He pulled back, glanced at his hand and then at her.

"Sorry. I'm one of those people who conducts a lot of electricity," she explained, trying to remember the last time she'd shocked someone on such a warm and humid day.

"I'll just bet you do." His comment was cryptic, but the deepened crease of two slashlike dimples told her he implied something sexual. Yet the fanciful glint disappeared quickly, leaving her to wonder if this man had just flirted with her or if her celibacy was finally driving her mad.

He gestured for her to lead the way, following a few steps behind when she opened the gold door across the hall, checked that the stairwell was empty and secure, then ushered him downstairs.

Leaving the Superdome without escort posed a greater threat now that a crowd had formed outside, so once they reached the lower level, Sam radioed for instructions. Tim Tousignant, the SuperMarketing Expo executive who'd also been caught in the crush, met them in the security office to ensure that Mr. LaRocca was indeed well and would return to give his presentation as soon as additional security measures were in place. Tim offered his personal limousine to deliver the Chicago food magnate back to his hotel, with Samantha as escort.

"I don't think that's necessary, Tim. The hotel is across the street," Dominick reasoned.

Tim shook his head, his face pinched and his gaze insistent. "There's a growing crowd out front. We'd just about calmed them down when something riled them again." He checked his watch, missing the look Dominick shot to Samantha. "The hotel lobby will be busy this time of day. Samantha can escort you through the service entrance." He turned his gaze directly on Sam. "See him safely to his room. I don't want his safety jeopardized again."

Samantha didn't like Tim's accusatory tone, but she bit back her sharp retort and nodded instead. She didn't figure Tim for the sass-me-and-get-away-with-it type. Like it or not, she needed this job until she could find something better—or until her brother-in-law and sister returned from Rio.

"I'll see to his safety."

Dominick shook his head, obviously chafing under the protective orders. "Miss Deveaux has been very effective, but I can manage on my own."

"I'm afraid I have to insist," Tim said, his tone conciliatory yet firm. "It won't be good business for the Expo if one of our top exhibitors is accosted outside the Superdome."

Nick eyed Samantha skeptically. Either he didn't trust her to do her job—which she doubted since the man didn't seem to be a fool—or he simply didn't want her around. She didn't blame him. As a bodyguard, resentment of her presence would be a common response. As nice and accommodating as her own childhood bodyguards had been, she'd disliked living under their watchful eyes from the day after her father's first megahit made him a celebrity, until she turned twenty-one and fired them herself.

Dominick's stare lasted a long moment, but then he nodded his acceptance of the inevitable. "Can you arrange tightened security by this afternoon?"

"I'll get right on it," Tim answered. "Samantha, radio Mitchell to send my driver around back. I apologize again, Mr. LaRocca. I had no idea..."

Dominick silenced the apology with a flattened palm. "Neither did I. Obviously, there's no accounting for some women's taste."

Self-deprecating humor looked good on him, Samantha decided, though if she hadn't already spent it, she'd bet next month's rent that he didn't employ such self-mockery often. Still, Dominick LaRocca seemed an interesting mix of contradictions. Gorgeous men like him didn't usually come in multidimensional models, at least not in her experience. Maybe there was more to him than met the eye.

Though the part that met the eye was pretty damn appealing.

While Dominick flipped open his cell phone to call his assistant before they left, Tim pulled her aside.

"Good job, Samantha. I didn't mean to jump on you. I just don't want Mr. LaRocca to think we take security lightly."

"No problem." She glanced at Tim's hand, still lingering on her elbow. He stepped back and shoved both hands into the pockets of his pressed and creased Armani slacks.

"Look, I know you took this job for the money. That's cool," Tim assured her, suddenly looking every inch the twenty-something marketing wunderkind he was. "Looks to me like Mr. LaRocca could use someone like your brother-in-law until this hype dies down."

Despite her many jobs, Samantha had never mastered the art of interviewing. At the time, she'd second-guessed her decision to be completely up front with Tim, but she was now impressed by his supportive attitude and excellent memory. He was probably trying to stave off any bad publicity, but Samantha sensed this wasn't the time for cynicism. "Thanks, Tim. But Brandon's still out of the country."

"If you say so." Then he winked. "I just thought you were dying to get your feet wet in the protection game yourself. You dipped your toe in today and did damned good. Remember that."

Tim nodded, then shook hands with Mr. LaRocca before jogging down the hall and back to work. Tim was a go-getter, all right. He'd moved up the corporate ladder by finding opportunities—not by waiting for them to find him, or worse, by waiting for some member of his family to hand him the brass ring. From the time her parents had divorced and she'd gone to California with her father, Sam had been programmed to put her life on hold until Devlin Deveaux found her focus for her. He'd cast her in her first film, guided her into stunt work, even had a major hand in her doomed relationship with Anthony.

For all intents and purposes, wasn't she now transferring that dependence from her father to her brother-in-law? Waiting for him to direct her?

Sam could indeed learn something from the way Tim's mind worked. Luckily, she was a quick study.

3

SAMANTHA INSISTED on stepping off the elevator first, trapping Nick and the two men from hotel security behind her. With her hand firmly flattened against his chest, she scanned the hallway. Nick knew she was just doing her job by keeping him from disembarking until she was convinced the path was clear, but he couldn't help grunting in frustration.

Even without a jolt of static electricity, her touch ignited an incendiary spark that he suspected would leave him with third-degree burns. Now was not the time for him even to *think*, much less fantasize, about a woman who's entire history and personal background hadn't been checked and double-checked. Thanks to his grandmothers, he was currently a hotter property than any man had a right to be. While he didn't intend to let the attention go to his head, he also wouldn't fall victim to some money-grubbing *femme fatale*.

Not that he had any reason to consider Samantha money-grubbing. But *femme fatale*? Oh, yeah. If she didn't remove her hand in the next few seconds, he was going to die a particularly slow and painful death from testosterone overload.

"Well?" he prompted, causing her to swing around, startled. His body instantaneously recalled the sensation of pressing against her and a pleasant heat stirred low in his groin, shooting sparks of sexual awareness to the tips of his fingers. She'd removed her hat when they entered the hotel, and her hair, a dark-blond hue that reminded him of the butterscotch sauce he loved to drench his ice cream with, fairly begged to be combed through. By him. In bed. After a champagne seduction and mind-blowing sex.

Which, unfortunately for both of them, wasn't going to happen.

"Deserted," she announced, tearing her hand away.

"No one to attack me? That's a switch." He dug his hands into his pockets and shrugged. But despite the bluster of his complaint, he didn't want to insult her again—or worse, sound conceited.

"Maybe you should recall all that pasta sauce," she teased. "Put a big fat tomato on the label instead."

He burrowed his fists deeper into his once carefully creased slacks. Amusement lit her eyes to the color of blue curaçao, a liqueur he could never refuse. "And sacrifice sales? Never. It's a small price to pay."

She shook her head. "Privacy comes with a big price tag in my book."

One of the hotel security guards who'd joined them in the elevator cleared his throat. Surprisingly, Nick had completely forgotten their presence. He was too busy trying to figure out why now, in the safety of this deserted hall, he didn't yet want Samantha Deveaux to return to her duties at the Superdome. He couldn't remember the last time someone had intrigued him so completely, especially someone without a single tie to the business he'd devoted his adult life to. The little socializing he did was either with family or friends, all in the restaurant or food business and all dependent on his expertise and business acumen to guide their futures.

Despite that they had nothing in common, he couldn't break the eye contact that held her still and kept him captive. She was like an infusion of fresh herbs in a dish laden with heavy cream. She not only added flavor to his morning, she lightened up the entire crazy experience. A glint shined from within her eyes, a sharp, focused gleam that reminded him of himself. At least, the self he was five or six years ago.

Lately, he reacted to the world with dour severity rather than with the relaxed, irreverent humor he'd once embraced—before he became Dominick LaRocca, the half-naked man on a pasta sauce label. Back when he was just Nick. The guy who hung out on Taylor Street. Who played stickball with the guys then flirted with the girls while they shared Italian Ices outside Mario's Lemonade Stand.

The guard behind him coughed again.

Without turning, Nick stepped off the elevator and sent them away. "Please see that your staff keeps my room number private."

Thus dismissed, the elevator door slid shut, followed by the mechanical whir of the descending cab.

"You want me to check out your room?" Samantha asked.

More than you know, he thought, marveling at this unexpected, invigorating attraction. She was *not* his type. For one, she spoke her mind whenever she wished. Women from his grandmothers to his cousin to his mother did exactly the same, without heed to his preference for feminine compliance and good old-fashioned peace and quiet. Second, she was too curvy. He preferred his women waiflike, willowy, even if they did threaten to break on any of the rare occasions where his passion flamed unchecked. Samantha Deveaux could clearly handle the unbridled, unhampered desire every man fantasized about.

"Actually, I thought I'd find Anita and determine when I could return to the Expo. You can coordinate the security plan before you leave."

She laughed while following him down the hall. "After our little fiasco this morning, I don't even know if I'll be employed by this afternoon."

"Tim seemed complimentary, when he thought I wasn't listening." He slid his card key into the gold box beside a double set of doors at the end of the hall.

She rewarded his covert eavesdropping with a sly smile. "Tim approved my hire, but he's in charge of the Expo, not the Dome. Maybe he has a lot of pull and won't let them fire me."

The lock clicked softly and he pushed the door open. "Fire you? Because you saved me from a crazed mob?"

"That mob should never have formed in the first place."

She dug her hands into her pockets, shuffling her feet, curling her bottom lip outward just enough to elicit exactly the correct amount of sympathy and guilt she obviously intended. Luckily for Nick, he'd dealt with more than enough scheming, conniving women in his lifetime to let her ploy work. And he'd thought her different from the women jumping onto the hood of his limousine or hiding in the mail cart at the office.

Yet, here she was, attempting to play him for a sucker with her tiny little frown and averted eyes. He should be disgusted, even disappointed.

Instead, he couldn't help but grin like a fool.

So she did want something after all. And for some reason completely at odds with logic or common sense, Nick couldn't wait to find out what.

"You're very good," he said. "Very convincing. The little lip thing is a perfect touch. I suppose now is when I offer to make a call on your behalf? Demand your promotion? A raise?"

"That's a bit much, but thanks. I have a better offer in mind." Samantha stepped in front of him, casing the room as she walked. Windows lined the curved foyer, leading past a wet bar to a large room with a conference table, six chairs, two fax machines, an active laptop computer and stacks of papers and LaRocca Foods brochures and promotional materials. Behind the table, a sitting area—complete with twin recliners, an overstuffed couch, a coffee table bearing the remnants of a room-service breakfast and an entertainment center—occupied the largest part of the room.

"Nice digs." She bit back asking if the door on the other side of the stored Murphy bed contained his bedroom or was just another exit into the hall. She'd already opened herself up to more than one sexual connotation this morning. Asking about his sleeping arrangements could prove unnecessary unless she convinced him to hire her as his private bodyguard.

"You don't want a promotion, huh? Hmm, let me think." He tossed his key onto the table and clicked the keyboard on his laptop, summoning the current stock-market statistics to flow across the bottom of the screen. "You did say this security job was temporary. Lay your proposal on the table, Samantha. I'm all ears."

"You need personal security. That's my gig."

"I thought your boss was out of town."

"He is. But we could still work out a mutually beneficial arrangement. You can hire me as your bodyguard—" she slipped around the entertainment center and glanced into the bathroom, which appeared to be empty "—at a discounted rate since I'm not yet fully licensed, and I'll make sure no one gets close enough to rip your clothes off."

"What's in it for you?"

"A chance to get out of this god-awful uniform."

He arched an eyebrow.

She frowned. She'd done it again. "You know what I meant."

"Actually, Samantha, I don't know. My grandmothers put more than my picture on that pasta label. In the small print, they listed my company position, the fact that I am still single and unattached, as well as a generous estimate of my net worth."

She pressed her lips together to contain another grin at his expense. "What were they trying to do, marry you off?"

His grim expression told her she'd hit the nail on the head.

"You're kidding!" And she thought her mother was bad, what with the gris-gris bags left on her doorstep and rows of candles lit at St. Louis Cathedral in hopes Samantha would finally find a man and settle down.

"Very ingenious women, your grandmothers." No hocus-pocus for them. Just good old-fashioned bribery. "They have a conduit to the general public, a product to sell—" she gestured toward him "—and at the same time, they increase sales by forty-six percent."

"Forty-seven," he corrected, not bothering to disguise his grouse as he tore off his striped tie and threw it on the couch.

"Forty-seven," she conceded, her gaze riveted as he twisted open the buttons at his collar. When he stopped at his breastbone, she glanced away, disappointed. Suddenly, she wanted another peek at that full-size pasta label, live and in person. "I'd like to meet your grandmothers sometime. But let's keep them away from my mother, okay? I don't want them giving her any ideas."

She motioned toward the bedroom door. He nodded his agreement to allow her search. No time like the present to demonstrate her diligence, especially when it would keep her from making a fool of herself by staring.

Flipping on the lights, she scanned the bedroom for unlawful entry and found none. The door to the outer hall, a secondary entrance so the room could be rented as a single when the suite was not in use, had an automatic lock. As far as she could tell, even the maid hadn't yet arrived. The bed, a rumpled storm of sheets and pillows, appeared untouched by anyone but Nick.

A copy of Mario Puzo's last hardcover lay on the nightstand, draped by a pair of thin gold, wire-rimmed glasses. Without much effort, she pictured the spectacles sitting on the bridge of Dominick's regal Grecian nose as he lay in bed, propped up by the half-dozen silky shams that littered the bed in sensuous disarray. Bare-chested, with a sheet draping him from the waist down, just enough to make her wonder exactly what, if anything, he wore to sleep...

"I bet you would."

She jumped at the sound of his voice. "Bet I would what?"

He leaned against the doorjamb, no less dressed than he was a moment ago, yet sinfully more sexy. "Want to meet my grandmothers?" He straightened, apparently misinterpreting the alarm on her face. "Do you see something out of place? Has someone been in my room?"

She shook her head, wondering if offering her services was a huge and horrible mistake. Here she thought she was immune to good-looking men like Dominick LaRocca. More like addicted, judging from her behavior so far. Standing in his bedroom, even one he'd rented for a few nights, heightened his presence. His cologne clung to the air. A damp towel, no doubt from his morning shower, was draped over a chair. A drawer in the dresser, not completely closed, cradled clothing that had once, or would soon, cling intimately to his skin.

"Everything looks fine." She slipped past him, holding her breath to keep from inhaling his scent when her shoulder touched his. "Except the maid service runs slow around here. I'll want to talk to hotel management about who they plan to send here and when." She stood beside his computer and crossed her arms over her chest. She simply needed to assume a more professional demeanor. If she was going to be an effective bodyguard, she had to stop thinking about his body.

"That's if I hire you," he reminded her with a boyish, mischievous wink that managed to clip her steady heartbeat.

Oh, no. She wasn't falling for his charm *that* easily.

"Why wouldn't you hire me? Because I'm a woman?"

Thankfully, he sat in one of the overstuffed chairs opposite the couch instead of joining her beside the conference table. Negotiations had begun and she needed the distance to think clearly.

"Precisely because you're a woman, and I don't mean that in the way you think. Don't you think your offer to protect me is a bit too convenient, in light of my circumstances?"

"You think I'm scheming to marry you?"

Sleep with you, maybe. Marry? Not in your wildest dreams, pal.

"A month ago, I'd expect to be slapped for such presumptuousness. But after being swarmed at the Expo, attacked at the airport and flashed by women wearing starched lace collars and prim business suits, nothing surprises me about the feminine gender anymore."

She nodded, understanding his reluctance. She was, after all, single and not totally invulnerable to his combustible combination of roguish good looks, power and charm. Hell, she'd have to be dead to ignore this man's Mediterranean magnetism. But despite her current need for a serious cash influx, his millions were probably a drop in the bucket compared to the return investment she'd receive from her father's next film.

"Have you ever heard of Devlin Deveaux?" she asked.

He repeated the name a few times. "Hmm. Hollywood type? Won some sort of award."

"His films have won twelve Golden Globes and he's been nominated for two Oscars."

"Oh, yes. The director. Does those action films. Why do you ask?"

"He's my father."

He stared at her blankly.

"He's *really* rich," she explained.

He still didn't get it.

She spoke slowly. "I don't need to marry for money."

He nodded, but smirked, obviously not convinced. "You don't have his money now, or you wouldn't be working as a security guard."

"True. I invested a hunk of cash in his next film and spent the rest moving back to Louisiana," she explained, leaving out the little detail that investing in Devlin's film was neither her idea nor her preference. Her father had once again found a way to keep her in his life through the money he owed her for her stunt work. "Once *Honor Guard* hits the theaters, I could end up with enough money to buy your company."

Her bravado inspired his quirky grin—one she instantly discovered she liked. A lot.

"The film-going public can be fickle," he pointed out.

"True again. But if this movie doesn't make it, his

next one will. The fact is, if I ever really needed to, I could ask my father for money. Or my mother. She's very comfortable. I don't need to sacrifice my freedom to live the high life, which, by the way, I don't want to live. Been there, done that. My interest in you is purely professional. My goal is to be a bodyguard, not a temporary security guard or, God forbid, someone's wife."

Dominick leaned back in the chair and assessed her coolly. "And you think my hiring an inexperienced bodyguard is a wise choice?"

She couldn't help admiring the pace of the man's thinking. He was quick, but so was she. "That inexperience saved you today, didn't it? I've been around celebrities all my life. I know what bodyguards do. I had my own bodyguard until I turned twenty-one. I'm a black belt in tae kwan do, I'm licensed to carry a concealed weapon and I have completed courses in threat assessment, security systems and access control."

He balanced his elbows on the armrests of the chair, steepling his fingers as he considered her speech. "You have a fine résumé, but what if I don't want a shadow wherever I go?"

"Better a shadow than potentially dangerous women."

He nodded, clearly still deliberating as he dialed Anita's cell phone and instructed her to find Tim Tousignant and tell him he needed Samantha until the Expo Hall was prepared for his rescheduled appearance at three o'clock. He then dialed room service and ordered fresh coffee.

He cupped his hand over the receiver. "Would you like anything?"

"Am I staying for lunch?"

"Your proposition has merits, but requires discussion."

"Do they have jambalaya on the menu?"

He asked and assured her they did.

"It probably isn't very good. Hotel food, you know."

He asked and assured her it would be excellent.

"I'll have the jambalaya."

He grinned, ordered two servings of jambalaya, a pound of steamed crawfish and a large hunk of praline cheesecake with sweet bourbon sauce.

"That's an awful lot of food for a man who just had breakfast." Especially for a man who looked like a walking, breathing advertisement for the local health club.

"I love food. It's not just business to me. Besides, that wasn't my breakfast. Anita ordered in."

Was Anita sharing his room? Samantha would have to know that, for entirely professional reasons, of course. "She's your assistant?"

"Yes, and my first cousin. Her father and my father are brothers."

He didn't need to add that tidbit of information, but Samantha found herself relieved that he did. She'd finally started to like the guy and didn't want it ruined by the knowledge that he slept with women he employed—as her father did, more times than she cared to count. When the last starlet started making stepmother noises, Samantha knew the time had come to split. She realized then that she'd spent her entire adulthood, not to mention a sizable chunk of her childhood, taking care of her father, catering to the genius director's whims and putting her interests second. Unfortunately, she'd only escaped as far as actor Anthony Marks's bed before he took his turn trampling her heart.

So now, she'd resolved to take care of strangers—on her own terms—and draw a salary at the same time. And she'd come home to New Orleans to reconnect with her mother and sister, both fiercely independent women that—with the exception of wanting her to find a man to settle down with—didn't attempt to run her life in any significant way. Coming home had been easier than she'd ever imagined, thankfully, since she'd never figured out how to work long-distance relationships. And she'd done her share of trying.

Dominick pulled a file folder off the coffee table onto his lap, then motioned for her to take a seat on the couch. "I like to start my day early. Anita's not a morning person, so she ordered her breakfast from here."

She slid a company brochure off the conference table behind her and flipped open the trifolded, high-gloss color pamphlet. On the cover, a posed crowd of over thirty people ranging in age from toddler to octogenarian lifted their glasses in a hearty *salute*. She recognized Anita just a little left of center, standing beside a woman who, judging by the resemblance, had to be her mother. Dominick was just behind her, bracketed by two gray-haired ladies holding tight to each arm—undoubtedly, his grandmothers, ensuring he stayed put for the photograph. The caption identified the crowd as LaRocca Foods, LaRocca Family.

She flashed the picture at him. "You've given a whole new meaning to the word *nepotism*."

"That's not nepotism." He picked up his own copy of the brochure from the corner of the table. "That's a family business. It's only nepotism if the family hired isn't qualified."

"Anita's good?"

His chin protruded with an adorable smidgen of pride, as if he was more than partially responsible for Anita's success. "The best. She loves this company almost as much as I do. Devotes her life to its success."

"Then why is she just your assistant and not a vice president of something?"

The nerve she hit must have been pretty darned raw, from the way his green eyes darkened to nearly black, and his scowl prickled gooseflesh along the back of her neck.

"She's in the position she's best suited for. Fancy titles don't mean anything."

"Oh, really? Then why don't you just call yourself a secretary? Or the maintenance guy?"

Nick's smile returned. "Actually, I tried mailboy once, but the paper cuts were hell."

Samantha sat back, shaking her head as the man effortlessly disarmed her indignation with unexpected humor. He was good. "I guess CEO does sound better, doesn't it?"

"Definitely. Tell me, is it part of your services as a bodyguard to stick your nose where it doesn't belong?"

"Only if it affects your safety."

"Then let's drop this subject. Anita isn't likely to be a threat to my safety."

She might be if you continue to undervalue her worth. For

once, Samantha kept her comment to herself. She'd already skated on thin ice with him and she quickly remembered that she wasn't his bodyguard—yet—and even if she were, he could send her packing without much cause.

"Sorry. I speak before I think way too often. It's just..."

"...a *lagniappe*? That's the word, isn't it?"

His tease caught her completely off guard. Not only did he know the popular New Orleans term for "something extra," but he considered her big mouth a bonus? One minute, he was all stern seriousness, the next he inspired a reluctant smile to tilt the corners of her mouth.

"Something like that. I'm not very familiar with the workings of close-knit families or family businesses. I have a lot to learn."

"What about filmmaking for the Deveaux? Did you ever work for your father?"

She returned her gaze to the brochure, perusing the lengthy list of products, from pasta sauces to salad dressings, his company produced. "Unfortunately, yes."

"You were an actress?"

An edge of distaste clung to his words, as if he eschewed the spotlight of celebrity as much as she did—which she honestly doubted. Men were men, after all. Most males she knew coveted the spotlight. Secretly lived for the sound of screaming fans and golden accolades. Even Dominick was currently mirrored in a life-size portrait across the street and on countless grocery aisles throughout the nation. "Small parts as a child, as an extra mostly. Then I did stunt work."

"That's very dangerous."

She shrugged, feeling a tenuous pull in the shoulder she'd dislocated on the set of *Blue Blood,* the film where she'd also earned a moderate concussion and two broken ribs. "That was part of the thrill, I guess."

"The thrill didn't last?"

When her stomach growled, she tossed the brochure onto the table. She hadn't eaten before work, and the enticing photos of steaming Italian delicacies had heightened her hunger. "Thrills rarely do."

"Depends on the nature of the thrill, don't you think?"

Suddenly, Samantha's hunger wasn't about food. His voice, already deep and throaty and hinting of that distinct Italian flavor that spiced his foods, dropped an octave and skirted on the edge of a whisper. Samantha's polyester uniform suddenly felt heavy, hot and binding, but she'd be damned before she let him know that.

"The newness wears off," she claimed, trying to stay on the topic of her former job as a stunt double, but succeeding in critiquing the sad progress of each and every relationship she'd ever found herself in. "Reality sets in. Fear comes into the picture and, bam, you're..." *Alone* "...out of work."

She glanced aside, careful to ignore the narrow assessment in his gaze.

"Being a bodyguard doesn't scare you?" he asked.

"Not so long as you promise not to fall off a fifteen-story building and stay out of cars wired to blow up when they hit their mark."

She flashed a smile meant to disarm his personal questions, but he deflected her attempt with a roll of his eyes and a shake of his head.

"I'll do my best. I suppose personal security is safer than stunt work."

"If the bodyguard is good and the subject is—" she knew better than to use the word *compliant* "—cooperative. The key to effective protection is threat assessment, followed by quick and decisive action. Combine that with collaboration with the subject, and a bodyguard has the easiest job on earth."

"Cooperation, huh? That could be a problem."

She snorted, not the least concerned that the sound was decidedly unattractive. With all the awareness crackling between them, she'd probably done herself a favor. "I've already factored that into my plan."

"Have you?"

She'd tossed her hat on the bar when she'd entered, but only now ran her fingers through her hair, wincing at the tangled mess. Standing, she caught her reflection in a nearby mirror and tried to work some order into the ponytail that had fallen apart.

"It's cool if you're a control freak, so long as you realize you'll have to throw some of that control my way to keep your privacy and safety intact."

More resigned than satisfied, she loosened the clip dangling at the nape of her neck, smoothed her hair back into place, secured the barrette and swung around. "One of those marriage-and-money-hungry women might be the if-I-can't-have-him-no-one-will types. Could get ugly."

He grabbed a pen from the table and jotted some figures into the margins of a contract as they talked. "That's your worst-case scenario?"

She laughed. "Nick, if you want worst-case scenarios, you'd better pour yourself a bourbon. I've got moviemaking in my blood. I can come up with some doozies."

He scribbled his signature on the highlighted lines, then closed the folder and tossed it back on the table. Clearing his throat, he leaned back into the chair and considered her from head to toe, nodding almost imperceptibly, as if satisfied with what he saw.

"Let's leave the fantasies to your father. My problem has escalated since I came to New Orleans."

"You didn't have problems in Chicago?"

"Back home, I know the turf and could take precautions. Here, I'm at a disadvantage. To add fuel to the fire, a few of the television newsmagazines picked up on the story of my grandmothers' marriage plan before I left. No doubt their reporters are lurking, though, thankfully, the Expo was closed to the media today. Which is precisely why I planned my presentation for today."

She leaned forward to retrieve the pen he'd tossed aside, along with a blank legal pad. "You mind?"

He shook his head. "I'm talking about a temporary assignment. The Expo ends on Sunday afternoon."

"Two days?" A decent chunk of change at the going rate, nothing to scoff at even with a discount. She'd at least be able to pay the rent on the office without running to either of her parents for cash. She calculated her cost in the margin. "I'm available."

"You'll have to quit your security job."

"Not exactly a problem."

"And it's not just the Expo I have to attend. I have several events around town—business meetings, dinners. A swamp tour with the president of our largest retailer. I'm not sure of the details. That's Anita's department."

Samantha frowned while she listed the scenarios she'd face. "Crowds will make it tough, but it can be done. I'll need your full itinerary, a phone and a place to work. I can put a plan together by this afternoon."

"Good. But I need a bit more than just a short-term plan. I'd like to tone things down before I return to Chicago. Answer some of the burning questions about my love life so those desperate women will crawl back into the woodwork."

He thought ahead. An admirable trait.

"Very smart. Make some kind of big splash here in New Orleans—employ the help of the media, even— make yourself old news by the time you go home. That's actually quite brilliant. You sound like my father's publicist."

"Thank you. I think. But..." He leaned forward in his chair, braced his elbows on his knees and looked up at her with a glint in his eye.

"But?" she prompted.

He wet his lips. "I'll need your help."

Samantha folded one leg beneath her, ready to spring off the chair. Something in his eyes told her to beware. Something in the fullness of his lips and tilt of his half smile triggered alarms in the deepest part of her belly.

"That's what you'll be paying me for."

"I'm not talking about hiring you as my bodyguard."

"What *are* you talking about?"

He moved from the chair to the edge of the coffee table, relieved her of both pen and pad and locked her hand into his. The studied, serious demeanor of the man who ran an empire melted away to leave only a man with eyes the color of emeralds and lips that could kiss a woman into unconsciousness.

"I'm talking about you, Samantha Deveaux. About hiring you not as my bodyguard, but as my lover."

4

NICK WATCHED Samantha's eyes. He'd wrangled enough tough negotiations to know that her initial reaction would map how he proceeded. Yet he almost felt like a novice going one-on-one with Samantha. She was tough, confident and sassy. And sexy. *Oh, yeah.* Sexy as sweet, silky oysters served with the finest Italian wine. Yet an elusive vulnerability lingered, teasing him like a secret. He didn't fool himself into thinking that recognizing her allure would counteract the mind-numbing effects. Women like her always had a trick up their sleeve.

Her thick-lashed lids narrowed. The irises he'd considered exotic, blue like a tropical liqueur, darkened to a fascinating, faceted sapphire, clear of any anger or insult from his purposefully bold, charged-by-design suggestion. In fact, he couldn't read her reaction at all. But, just in case, he held her hand tightly, prepared to deflect a slap.

When she glanced down, he realized that Samantha Deveaux didn't have to use her hands to punish his presumptuous proposition. She shifted her knee ever so casually.

Fortunately for his family jewels, she had a sense of humor to go with her proclaimed black belt. Her expression turned from cool to amused, forcing him to replay the words in his head one more time. He'd been trying to disarm her with an outrageous idea, but his words rang a little too cocky and arrogant, even for him.

She obviously didn't seem to mind. By the time he released her hands with a groan, she was laughing out loud. Which knocked his naturally bred arrogance down a substantial peg.

"I didn't mean that exactly the way it sounded," he said, grumbling.

"I should hope not. I mean, do I look like Julia Roberts in this get up?" She took a deep breath to tamp down her laughter. "'Cause you, pal—" she pointed for emphasis "—ain't Richard Gere."

Nick met her smirk with a reluctant, albeit agreeing grin. No, he wasn't Richard Gere. He never wanted to be Richard Gere or any other celebrity for that matter. He just wanted to run the family business and turn their healthy profits into steady millions. He wanted to expand the product line. Make LaRocca a household word for pasta sauce like Kleenex was for facial tissue. Ensure that everyone who shared his blood had a chance at a prosperous future.

Since his appointment as CEO, he'd schemed and planned and jockeyed to put his company, relatively small and still privately operated, into the leagues where only conglomerates dared to tread. Big dreams, but he was so close to achieving them. He just needed more time—more single, unattached, undistracted-by-a-wife time.

Samantha could buy him his needed reprieve. And maybe a little excitement, too. Excitement that had been sorely lacking in his life for way too long, a reality this sexy security guard effortlessly proved.

"If I'm going to get any business done, I need a bodyguard," he said, determined to clarify his point. "You've convinced me of that. If we lead everyone to believe that we are an item, that would give you a reason to be with me all the time, which would..."

She nodded as she took over his sentence, her laughter dying as business encroached. "...save your big male ego from admitting you need protection."

"Yes, well," he admitted, wondering how this stranger knew him so well in less than an hour's time, "my big male ego does sometimes need saving, but I have a higher payoff in mind. If the public believes that I'm no longer available...that half of my net worth will soon be spoken for..."

Sam applauded. "Nice twist. You convince all those single women that you've made your choice, and they set their sights on the next rich bachelor." After a moment, she wrinkled her nose. "But you know, if I'm going to play your bimbo for the whole world to see, I think I'll rescind the discount offer. We'll call it danger pay. I do have a reputation to protect."

Nick grinned. He'd had no idea that Samantha would be so easy to convince. She either seriously needed the money or she didn't want to wait to become a bodyguard. Either reason, he respected her lack of self-doubt.

They were two peas in a pod. Which added a layer of protection to his plan. Nick might no longer be entirely clear on the kind of woman he *really* wanted to marry someday, but he was quite certain he didn't want a woman who operated exactly the way he did. Career first, money second, reputation third—and in a succession that ran so close, the distinction between each goal was acutely hard to decipher.

"Samantha Deveaux has a reputation?" He hummed his interest, wiggling his eyebrows to make sure he needled her sufficiently. "It's been a long time since I hung out with a girl who had a rep. One of the DiCarlo sisters, if I remember correctly." Now wasn't the time to point out that he never had and still did not date "bimbos." Even the DiCarlo sisters back in high school had just been looking for a little harmless fun. But he didn't want Samantha to think that he rarely dated anymore, true or not. And he'd expect such an assumption. Why else would his grandmothers have stirred the wild single masses in the first place?

Unfortunately, Nick couldn't remember his last date. He'd broken off his engagement to Sophia over two years ago, and hadn't seen anyone else since, first out of respect for Sophia and then because he didn't have the time. Dating required way more effort than he was willing to expend, especially since he no longer knew what he wanted.

He'd dated a lot during college, but as soon as his company went public seven years ago, he'd met Blair, the sophisticated daughter of a Chicago entrepreneur who should have understood his devotion to business pursuits, but didn't. She was too cool, too calculating and required way more attention than he had time to give. Sophia, a friend from the old neighborhood, should have been perfect. She embraced all the traditional values he thought he treasured. She ended up driving him crazy and he doubted he was any picnic for her either.

He suspected Samantha Deveaux would drive him crazy, too, but in an entirely different, entirely desirable way.

"So tell me about this reputation of yours," he said. "I'm utterly intrigued."

Samantha stood, her lips pressed tight but her eyes smiling. "I'll bet you are. But," she said with a sigh, "this is the unfair part of the protection game. I get to know everything about you and my life is off limits."

Nick had no idea if she realized that she'd just issued a delicious challenge, but he guarded his expression. He nodded as if he agreed to her terms.

One quick call to his attorneys, who would in turn contact their private investigation division, could garner him each and every detail of Samantha Deveaux's life within an hour or two. If he gave them a whole day, the high-priced sharks he kept on retainer could write her biography, complete with photographs of her twelfth birthday and an interview with her third-grade boyfriend.

But damn, it would be so much more fun to discover her secrets himself.

A knock at the door gave him pause to wonder what the hell he was doing toying with his new bodyguard when he had work to do. He started to answer the door when Sam placed her hand on his shoulder, popping him with another electric shock.

"Ow!" he said, exaggerating the pain, but not the intensity of her touch.

"Sorry." She snatched her hand back and shoved it

in her pocket. "I don't know what's up with me today. I'm not usually this electric."

Oh, I doubt that. "You should work for a hospital. You'd save them a bundle on defibrillators."

She merely grinned but she might as well have stuck out her tongue. He swallowed a chuckle.

"It's too soon for room service," she said. "Let me answer the door." She straightened her unwrinkled uniform before she disappeared around the corner.

Nick sank into the chair, wondering what the hell was coming over him. Yeah, his plan had a damn good chance of working. A few high-profile photographs of him and Samantha together, perhaps with her wearing a great big flashy ring, and the novelty of his grandmothers' scheme might die a quick death. He couldn't imagine there was a woman alive who'd want to compete with Samantha Deveaux for his attention. At least not a sane woman.

He could only hope that sane or insane, those women who'd been compelled to buy his products because of the *Playgirl* label would actually taste some of his grandmothers' secret recipe and be won over. The last thing any of them intended was to lose business because he was getting married.

Which he wasn't. Getting married. Not really.

He clapped his hand on his forehead. The stereotypical Italian phrase *Mama mia!* rang loud and clear, even if he'd never actually heard any Italians he knew say it. Fact was, the sentiment fit.

He could at least take comfort in knowing that Samantha Deveaux would provide ample protection from any more crazed single women intent on capturing his attention and ripping off his clothes. It wasn't so easy to concentrate on business with women baring their breasts in his face and snatching at his crotch. He entertained no fantasies that Samantha would bare or snatch. At least not without *a lot* of encouragement on his part, which he most certainly couldn't afford to give. Maybe he'd finally be able to forget about this mess and concentrate on the European distribution deal.

Too bad all he seemed able to concentrate on was Samantha.

That baffled him. She was *so* not his type. She was neither reserved and icy, like Blair had been, nor quiet and demure like Sophia. He'd once had high hopes for both relationships—if he'd only had time to pursue them. But Blair ended up being way too high maintenance and Sophia too clingy. He couldn't concentrate on business with them around.

And unlike today, he hadn't been distracted from a stack of contracts or a pile of phone messages by thoughts of hot, sweaty sex with a woman who carried handcuffs on a daily basis.

No, the distraction Samantha offered was entirely different from his issues with his former lovers.

Blair had constantly interrupted him at the office to show him the booty from her latest shopping spree. To share some inane gossip. To fill his calendar with social events more boring than waiting for his grandmothers to play their ritual game of canasta before every board meeting to determine who banged the gavel.

Sophia, on the other hand, had called once a day at precisely the same time to remind him that she was home, waiting to do whatever he wanted her to do, whenever he wanted her to do it. She bought his socks and had his shirts ironed. She attended family gatherings and dutifully sent out all his birthday, anniversary and condolence cards until she'd so endeared herself to the family that their breakup had nearly caused a holy war.

Never again, he'd promised himself. He was better off alone, he'd decided. Until his grandmothers issued their ultimatum.

Until Samantha Deveaux hurtled into his life.

He listened as Samantha argued and denied entrance to whoever was at the door. He stood up and stepped into the hall when he heard a suspicious creak in the adjoining bedroom.

"I told you, we didn't order filet mignon," Samantha insisted. "You just wait right here...Jimmy...while I call down to room service and get this cleared up."

"Oh, no, ma'am. Please. I'm on, like, probation with the hotel. I can't mess up again."

He imagined her sapphire eyes narrowing with suspicion. "Then why don't you sneak back downstairs, get our correct order and come back up?"

"Um-um..."

Samantha seemed to have the stuttering waiter under control, so when he heard the rustle of material from within his bedroom, he decided to investigate himself. Probably just the maid entering through the side door, he thought. The side door he'd instructed the hotel *not* to use.

He stopped just outside the bedroom door. He didn't have to be a rocket scientist to realize this was precisely the type of situation where he should alert Samantha and let her investigate. The thought turned his stomach more than he expected, churning up the humiliating memory of being nine years old and spooked by a celebrity who'd brought his entourage to the family restaurant for dinner. He'd hidden behind his mother's apron. Literally. The sickening swirl of hot embarrassment coursed through him again, as if the incident hadn't happened twenty-five years ago.

It didn't help that his cousins, uncles, father and grandfather loved to retell the story at each and every family gathering—or whenever they suspected the power of running the business had gone to his head. It also didn't help that, yet again, his life was being molded and shaped by a woman. First his mother, then his Nanas, and now, in a sense, by Samantha.

He pushed into his room. The door, a side entrance into a private hallway, was locked and bolted from the inside. He didn't remember doing that, but guessed Samantha had taken that precaution when she'd searched the room. He glanced at the bed and then to the closet. Nothing seemed amiss. He was going crazy, that was all. Certifiably nuts.

"What's wrong?"

Samantha appeared behind him and reached forward, then pulled her hand back before she shocked him again. Thank God.

"Nothing," he answered, berating himself for being so jumpy over what was probably the sound of the air conditioner kicking on. "Who was that at the door?"

Sam shook her head and pursed her lips, a habit she had that he sorely wished she'd break. All that pink softness puckered and primed was the last thing he needed to see every time she had a deep thought. Which was way too often for a woman as beautiful as she was.

"He *said* he was from room service," she answered.

"You didn't believe him?"

"His jacket was too big and he was incredibly nervous. And he got the order completely wrong, as if he'd swiped the cart. This is a Hyatt. They may forget the ketchup every once in a while, but they don't screw up that royally, especially not on an order for a VIP suite. I got rid of him, but I'll call down and check it out."

He expected her to head for the phone, but instead she stepped closer. Her hand lingered near his arm so that he could feel the charged crackle that seemed to emanate from her fingertips.

"You sure you're okay?"

He cleared his throat. He wasn't anywhere near okay. He was distracted, disheveled, and now, apparently, paranoid. "Why?"

"Because you look like this." She mirrored his cranky expression—furrowed brow, narrow eyes and grumpy chin.

He couldn't help but laugh out loud. "God, I hope not. I'll never sell another jar of pasta sauce again if that expression's on the label."

She backed away, somewhat flustered, if he could believe that anything or anyone could fluster Samantha Deveaux.

"Well," she said, "there's always the big fat tomato."

THERE'S ALWAYS the big fat tomato? Not exactly the most witty response she could have come up with, but with Nick switching from dangerously worried to laughing with a sexy rumble that still reverberated straight to her toes, it was the best she could do.

She hurried to the phone and dialed the restaurant that handled room deliveries. The hotel did employ a waiter named Jimmy, but not only was he off for the day, he was pushing sixty and African-American. Definitely not the barely twenty-year-old Caucasian who'd shown up. She dialed the hotel manager immediately. He insisted on bringing their order up himself and assured her that hotel security would search for the impostor without delay.

She hung up the phone, reeling. This was a real job. A *real* bodyguard assignment. Mr. Dominick LaRocca, multimillion-dollar CEO, was honestly and truly being stalked. By a twenty-year-old *male*, no less. She doubted marriage was on the kid's mind, making her wonder what he'd wanted by trying to weasel into Nick's room.

The possibilities were endless. And damn exciting.

But not nearly as exciting as watching Nick march around the conference table, tapping the keyboard on his laptop without sitting first, flipping open files, stacking and reorganizing papers as if the survival of the world depended on his next deal.

The thrill took a decidedly cooling turn when she remembered who he reminded her of.

"My father never sits when he works either," she said, once again saying something aloud that she meant to bemuse privately.

"Your father is an extremely successful man. I'll take the comparison as a compliment."

"You would," she said with a laugh.

He stopped, letting a thick file slap back onto the polished table. "What does that mean?"

Anita's voice intruded. "She means that you're an arrogant SOB. Or maybe *conceited* is a better word."

Samantha watched Anita pocket her key as she rounded the corner of the long foyer. Sam needed to get her mind back in the game. She should have heard Anita come in, even if the woman was shoeless and had her own key.

"Samantha has only known me for an hour. Takes at least two before my conceit truly shows," Nick said matter-of-factly, though he winked playfully at Samantha, causing another surge of blood flow from her heart to her outer limbs.

Anita waved her hand at him. "She'd only have to know you for about two minutes to figure out that your head is bigger than the vats we cook our marinara in."

"She loves me, can't you tell?" Nick strode to Anita, spun her around for a quick once-over, then kissed her on the cheek and went back to his paperwork. "The barefoot look is interesting. Trying to start a fashion trend?"

Anita swore when she noticed a hole in her panty hose. "Very funny. If you don't get married soon, I may end up in the hospital after another riot like today's. Maybe you should do a talk show or something. If those women knew how boring you were, they wouldn't be so hot to marry you."

Samantha watched and listened. She'd known Dominick LaRocca for only a brief time, but she'd never describe him as dull. Or predictable. She'd already made the incorrect assumption that he didn't appreciate women like her who voiced their opinions without hesitation—good, bad or insulting. Apparently, he liked Anita a whole lot. Sam did, too. His cousin apparently practiced less diplomacy than Sam did, which could keep Sam out of trouble for once in her life.

"Crazy to marry me?" Nick asked. "I'd say they're just crazy. This is Samantha Deveaux, by the way," he introduced.

Anita accepted Samantha's offered hand.

"Anita LaRocca. Thanks for jumping in back there. If you hadn't removed the meat from the feeding frenzy..." Anita glanced over her shoulder to wait for Nick's objection to her metaphor, but he ignored her. She shrugged. "Anyway, I lost a perfectly matched pair of sling-back Monolos and our supply of presentation folders in the fray, but fortunately—" she patted her long dark curls "—no clumps of hair this time."

"This time?"

"Didn't Nick tell you about the airport?"

"Not exactly."

"Let's just say that the woman who nearly commandeered our limousine last night mistook me for Nick's girlfriend and tried to make me look like Sinéad O'Connor."

"It might have been a good look for you, Anita," Nick offered, though he'd appeared to be ignoring them while he dialed about twenty-five numbers into the phone.

"Well, you won't have to worry anymore," Sam assured her. "Nick's hired me to provide protection for him." She tugged on her uniform. "This security-guard gig was temporary. I also work for No Chances Protection, a local bodyguard service."

Anita blinked, wide-eyed. "Oh, really?"

"You don't approve?" Sam asked, unable to interpret Anita's arched eyebrows and slightly agape mouth.

She shook her head. "Approve? I think it's great. Hell, with you following him around, no one will notice me. Especially if you ditch the uniform. You know..."

Anita's dark eyes, saucer-shaped and chocolate brown, widened as an idea struck her. She raised her finger to preface her brilliant pronouncement, when Nick hung up the phone.

"We're one step ahead of you. Samantha has agreed to ditch the uniform and play my girlfriend for the next few days."

The exchange between the cousins was nearly nonverbal as Anita slapped her hands together triumphantly and beat a path to the phone. They apparently shared the same wavelengths and thought patterns, but Samantha suspected their intentions meshed on the surface only. She distinctly remembered Nick telling her that Anita has been a coconspirator in his grandmothers' scheme. Notwithstanding her desire to keep all her hair attached to her head and her five-hundred-dollar shoes intact, Anita's instantaneous excitement over their scheme made Sam incredibly suspicious.

Rude though it might have been, Sam listened intently to each and every word of Anita's phone call.

"Nana Rose? Hi! How's everything going?...uh-huh...give her a kiss for me. Okay. Yeah. Listen, did you hear? You did...Rick from Sales called? Yeah, not surprised. No, we're both fine. This beautiful security..." Anita tossed a glance over her shoulder at Samantha while her grandmother apparently interrupted the rest of the story. "Yeah. Blond, late-twenties, athletic. Very pretty...no, probably not Italian...but...uh-huh...yeah, I'll let you know what happens...okay. *Ciao.*"

Anita chuckled as she hung up the phone, but Sam couldn't contain a frown. She didn't like to be talked about. She never had. Especially by some scheming Italian grandmother who, despite being hundreds of miles away in Chicago, already knew what had happened at the Dome only an hour ago.

"Let me guess," Nick said, amused. "They'd already heard a full report."

"Thanks to Rick, the suck-up," Anita said with a disbelieving nod. "And here I thought I was their best spy."

"So, what do they think?" The sheer interest in Nick's gaze denoted the importance of his cousin's conversation with their grandmother. Made sense. If the Nanas didn't buy that Nick was genuinely interested in Samantha, the ruse wouldn't work. The grandmothers were the first line to the press and the general public, and Samantha surmised that these women weren't pushovers. Women didn't found and run multimillion-dollar companies by being easily fooled.

Anita turned back toward Samantha and took a step forward as if she planned to circle and assess Samantha's suitability before answering. Suitability for what, Sam didn't care to know. She stopped Anita with a pointed stare, so Nick's cousin slid into a chair instead.

"She's not Italian," Anita said, twisting her mouth as if Sam's heritage was a stumbling block to success. "Are you?"

"Not according to my mother, no." Sam shoved her hands into her back pockets. "My heritage is completely Creole, French-Canadian with a touch of Spanish, I believe, though what it has to do with my ability to be Nick's bodyguard, I don't understand."

"But you're not going to be just his bodyguard, now, are you?"

Samantha squirmed. She hadn't minded Nick's plan so much when it was just his idea, presented with his cool logic and clear desire to rid himself of his celebrity-bachelor status. Anita's gaze was entirely too ripe with unspoken schemes and possibilities. Schemes that went way beyond fooling the public, especially now that the infamous Nanas were involved.

Samantha crossed her arms. "That's exactly what I'm going to be. A bodyguard. Period. The rest will just be a cover. It'll help me navigate through his appearances, and if it helps him with his problem, that's fine, too. But..." Sam felt odd saying more in front of Nick, but she had no choice. "But don't get any ideas that this is more than an illusion. A ruse to take the heat off your cousin."

Anita nodded way too complacently. "Oh, of course.

It's all a sham. But it's brilliant. And could definitely benefit us all."

A knock on the door once again broke the tension. Nick returned his attention to the laptop; Anita grabbed a pen and paper and started scribbling. Samantha marched to the door to greet the hotel manager, accompanied by a tray that proved to contain their correct lunch order.

Unfortunately, she wasn't hungry anymore.

She rolled the cart to where Anita and Nick now leaned over a spreadsheet of tiny numbers and graphs.

She cleared her throat. "Lunch is served. Hotel security is parked in front of your door until I get back. Don't leave this room without an escort."

"Where are you going?" Nick asked, eyeing the cart that he'd ordered for them. Luckily, Anita was there to enjoy her food for her. Sam knew there was no way in hell she would eat a bite until she stopped her head from spinning and her stomach from churning.

Incredible reactions, both of them. She could jump off a fifteen-story building with barely an accelerated heartbeat. But playing lover to Nick LaRocca? A heart attack was surely imminent.

"To give my notice at the Dome, change clothes and finalize all the arrangements for your appearance at your booth this afternoon. I'm sure Tim will help me work out the details. Then I'll be back."

Anita was already lifting the metal lids off the food and making yummy noises over the cheesecake. "You sure you don't want to stay and eat?"

"No, really. Go ahead. I have work to do."

Better to act and sound efficient if she wanted to

command respect for her protection skills, she decided. Luckily, her drama talents weren't as rusty as she might have guessed.

Before she'd even left the room, Nick and Anita were muttering about cost projections and shelf space as if she'd never been there. *Good*. An effective bodyguard had to become invisible when the situation warranted.

Too bad she hadn't thought about that an hour ago, when Nick LaRocca crowded into her life.

5

"How did you luck out and find her?" Anita asked the moment the door clicked behind Samantha.

Nick shook his head as he grabbed a steaming bowl of jambalaya and napkin-wrapped utensils from the cart. "You said it—pure luck."

Luck and something Nick could only describe as poetic justice. Here he was avoiding single, attractive women as if he were under consideration to be chosen as pope, and the most irresistible female he'd met in years rescues him from disaster. "When she offered her services as a bodyguard, I thought I'd try a different tactic to beat Nana Rose and Nana Fae at this little marriage game they've concocted."

Anita ignored the spicy rice and crawfish that he'd ordered and went straight for dessert. "You should know better than to try and beat them, Nicky. They've been around too long. They know all the angles." She dug her fork into a huge hunk of cheesecake, swirled the ivory triangle into the caramelized bourbon sauce and then slid the sweet morsel in her mouth with a loud groan. "This is delicious!" Her words were muffled by her mouthful. "We should do desserts. I've always said we should do desserts."

"Don't change the subject," Nick insisted, accustomed to the turn in Anita's focus. His cousin had a sweet tooth the size of the Sears Tower and, like him, she had trouble separating business from pleasure. "I'm going to need your help to make this work. No double-agent crap this time." He pointed his fork at her while she licked hers clean, swallowing a chuckle as her brown eyes darkened to nearly black.

For a brief instant, he wondered what he'd have to serve to darken Samantha's eyes that way. More than cheesecake, he'd bet. But before he could imagine the details, he shook the thought away.

"Are you with me, or with them?" he demanded.

Anita immediately skewered another bite of cheesecake, avoiding his stare while she hummed her gastronomic pleasure. Nick knew he was playing dirty, making his cousin choose between her loyalties to their grandmothers and her loyalty to him, but he didn't have a choice. If she blabbed that Samantha was only his bodyguard and not his lover, his plot would be ruined. He wouldn't get a better chance to divert the unwanted attention on his marital status back to the quality of LaRocca Foods' products. Getting to know Samantha better at the same time was just another stroke of luck.

"Anita? I need to know. Right now."

She sliced into her cheesecake again, but kept the morsel balanced on her fork. "It's too late to issue ultimatums, Nicky. I already know your plan. I could blab right now."

"You could have blabbed on the phone a few minutes ago, too. But you didn't. Can I take that as an 'I'm with you, Nick?'"

Nick knew she'd only gone along with their grandmothers' label scheme more as a practical joke than because she had any real interest in whether or not he got married. She knew that the future of the company, and consequently her future, rested in his hands.

If this plan failed, the corporation could end up broken into so many small companies that even *if* Anita were given one to run, her chances of achieving true success would be next to nothing. Not that his cousin wasn't smart or savvy enough to run a business. She just wouldn't have the capital to break out of the pack. Slowly, big food conglomerates would swallow each division. The LaRocca products would become homogenized and lose the homegrown charm and authentic appeal that made them a success in the first place.

He wouldn't let that happen.

And he bet Anita wouldn't either. And though he also knew his grandmothers didn't want that outcome, they wouldn't live forever. He had to convince them to change their minds about making his marital status an issue or he'd lose the business for sure.

"Unless you don't want me to continue as CEO?" he asked, trying not to sound as arrogant as Anita constantly accused him of being. Arrogance didn't drive him this time; confidence did.

Anita sighed. "You know I want you at the helm, Nicky, but our Nanas do have a point about this diehard bachelor status of yours. This line you give them about holding out for a nice quiet wife with no opinions of her own is a load of bull. Sophia was *exactly* that woman and you couldn't wait to break free of her."

"Sophia was too clingy," he snapped, knowing the

distinction was tenuous. "She wanted my approval on what dry cleaner to pick. What laundry detergent to use."

"No opinions of her own," Anita said, shaking her head. "Just like you ordered."

Nick stirred his rice. An aromatic steam drifted from his plate, promising a kaleidoscope of flavors that might undo his increasingly foul mood. He dug in his spoon. "Next time, I'll make my order more specific. No opinions of her own *about me and my life.* And she can pick her own damn laundry detergents."

Anita shook her head as she grabbed two goblets of ice water from the room-service cart. "Sooner or later, you'll have to settle down with someone. You love family way too much to stay single forever."

"I could say the same for you," he countered.

"But you won't." She stabbed her fork in his direction. "You know damn well that if I get involved with a man, I won't be available 24-7 to run your life."

"If I get roped into marriage, maybe I won't need you to run my life."

She was incredibly quiet and expressionless while she chewed and swallowed. "Don't tease me with pipe dreams. Look, you know I think you're the best person to run LaRocca Foods. Nana Rose and Nana Fae think so, too. But you need a life beyond the business. Although I only met her for a minute, I like Samantha Deveaux. I'd hate for her to get hurt in any of this."

Though Nick knew Samantha was as different from Sophia as sugar was from salt, he couldn't squash the memory of Sophia's teary-eyed departure from his life, the love letters she'd sent for weeks after he'd told her their relationship was over. He hadn't meant to—hadn't intended to—but he'd hurt her nonetheless. The only thing that had saved him from a lifetime of guilt was knowing she'd become engaged to Anita's brother, Carmine, less than two months later. Carmine was a softhearted, attentive man who put business second and his happiness first. It didn't help make him top sales rep for the southeast division, but he'd probably win Husband of the Year.

And though Samantha was as different from Sophia as she was from Blair Davenport—who'd reacted to his breakup by shrugging her shoulders, kissing him coldly and moving immediately along to a richer, more powerful CEO—he doubted Sam would fall victim to any man, much less him. She had a strength about her, a nearly-but-not-quite jaded outlook that would probably keep her heart effectively insulated.

"You don't need to worry about my bodyguard. Her interests are purely professional. She seems entirely immune to my charm."

Anita cracked a grin. "You have charm?" She chuckled at her own quip before finishing off her cheesecake in three quick bites. "Okay, I'm stuffed. Time to hit the workout room."

"No way," Nick protested. "You need to put together some new presentation folders, make an anonymous call to the press about my chance meeting with the security guard who saved me, and then wait here for Sam's call to finalize the logistics for my appearance at the Dome. You only have a couple of hours."

He slipped his spoonful of jambalaya into his mouth, groaning with pleasure at the sudden burst of spicy flavors and diverse textures on his tongue—hot cayenne pepper, sweet rice, chunky sausage. He'd had Cajun food back home in Chicago, but it just wasn't the same. Something about this city, even cooped up in a hotel room thirty stories above the ground, communicated a festive atmosphere of sights and sounds—plastic beads, gold coins and hot jazz.

Of course, he felt quite certain that his run-in with New Orleans-born Samantha Deveaux had something to do with his romanticism. She may not have been raised in the city, but she summoned her drawl on command, walked with an innate rhythm and evoked alluring images he'd forever associate with the Crescent City.

Anita slid her plate, practically licked clean, back onto the cart. "What are you going to do while I'm working my fingers to the bone?" she asked, protesting more out of habit than because she resented the tasks he'd just assigned.

"I'm going to finish this delicious jambalaya, then change into a suit that isn't torn."

She eyed him skeptically. "That'll take a few hours?"

He chewed his next bite slowly, relishing the taste of the Cajun concoction the same way another man might enjoy a kiss. He didn't have much experience with kisses lately, but if the act could prove half as hot as his lunch, he might actually try to change that fact.

Samantha's generous lips, pursed and thoughtful, immediately popped into his mind.

Anita cleared her throat to remind him she'd asked a question. He had planned, after eating lunch and choosing a new suit, to spend a few hours finishing his memo to the marketing department regarding their presentation to the European distributor. But with Samantha on his mind, his body wouldn't be satisfied by just a hearty lunch. Anita had given him a better idea.

"I think I'll take your spot in the workout room."

"Pig," Anita snapped, then laughed and shook her head with resignation. "I don't know...Samantha told you not to go anywhere, and even with an escort, you'll be half-dressed and sweating in the gym. It's a public place. You could start another stampede."

Nick smiled to acknowledge her teasing lilt but, unfortunately, she wasn't entirely wrong. Still, he needed an outlet to burn off his sudden surge of energy or he'd never manage to appear cool and in control when Samantha returned.

"Then call the hotel manager and arrange for a step machine to be brought to the room. I've *got* to exercise."

Anita pushed away from the table, her smile entirely too smug. "I don't suppose shapely Samantha Deveaux has anything to do with your need to pump something, does it?"

That settled it. He and Anita spent *way* too much time together. His cousin could read him like a book in most situations, so she'd know to back down if he barked loud enough.

"Just get me the equipment."

"Yes, sir." She saluted, grabbed her glass of ice water and retired to the desk tucked in the corner of the room, out of his way.

Good. He liked a woman who knew when to back down.

Unfortunately, he doubted Samantha Deveaux possessed that particular talent. If she, for whatever reason, did turn her sights on him, he'd be lost for sure.

"I'M BORROWING your purple suit." Samantha tucked the phone beneath her chin and used both hands to pull the outfit out of her sister's overstuffed hall closet. She wobbled and recovered, stepping over Serena's sheepdog, who'd parked his wide, half-asleep body in front of the door.

"I own a suit?" Serena asked from the other end, thousands of miles away, her voice crackling in and out from a beach in Brazil.

"Apparently so." Samantha pulled a name tag off the slim lapel. "You wore it to some convention."

"Oh, yeah. I have to warn you, it's not very professional. The skirt is short—really short—and the jacket doesn't take a blouse."

Sam sighed as she laid the creation in question over the guest-room bed, her sister's assessment ringing true even while she heard her new brother-in-law making some sexy comment in the background. She'd have nowhere to hide her gun in this getup. She'd have to opt for a purse, which would slow her response time if things got hairy.

"There's more material in a bath towel than this outfit," Sam said. "Why did you buy it? It's not your style at all." Not that her sister dressed the least bit conservatively. Serena favored long, sexy sarong skirts, tie-dyed tank tops and lots and lots of noisy jewelry. But while her mode of dress was alluring, the breeziness denoted a casual nonchalance that matched Serena's sensual personality perfectly. This suit was way more overt. More *here I am.*

More like their mother.

"I didn't buy it, Mother did," Serena confirmed. "She swapped my suitcase on the way to the airport for the convention. Left me a seduce-me-quick wardrobe. You'll find an interesting collection of miniskirts, low-cut blouses and ridiculously high heels in that closet."

"You kept them?"

"What else was I going to do? Donate them to some charity for streetwalkers?"

Sam chuckled. She hadn't really looked at the other outfits, but while this suit was indeed short and snug, she doubted any hookers would be interested. A high-priced call girl? That was another matter.

"You know Mother," Serena continued, her tone half-frustrated and half-bemused. "She was hoping I'd go to Vegas and catch me a man. You should see the lingerie she bought to go with that stuff."

"Didn't you take it on your honeymoon?" Sam teased.

"Are you kidding? She bought me a whole new collection for my trousseau. The old stuff's in the mahogany chest of drawers next to the window. They're all yours if you want them. Never been worn."

Samantha eyed the dresser in the corner, but rooted her feet to the floor. She'd never taken an interest in sexy lingerie before. She thought they were pretty and whiled away her share of time thumbing through catalogs, but her lifestyle demanded sports bras for support and thongs that wouldn't show through her wardrobe. And the men in her life hadn't minded.

But meeting Nick, touching Nick—even briefly—had initiated a sudden fascination with peek-a-boo lace and slick, silky satin. He seemed like a man who would appreciate the extra touch of femininity, the hint of romance.

She took a few steps toward the mahogany chest, and then glanced back at the outfit she'd chosen from her sister's closet. The fleeting image of her wearing a scant and sensual silk panty beneath the minuscule suit while sharing space with Dominick LaRocca filled her with a mixture of excitement and wantonness that she hadn't felt in a long, long time. And with good reason. In the past, Samantha's libido had often overrode her common sense. She had to squash this attraction soon, or her bodyguard assignment would prove more torturous than exciting. Unfortunately, she knew of only one effective way to derail sexual tension.

Sex. And that was out of the question.

Wasn't it?

"Don't you have anything more conservative?" Samantha asked into the phone, begging for a reprieve from what just might be inevitable.

"I have the black dress I wore to Cousin Arthur's funeral."

Sam shook her head and shivered. "The one with the ostrich-feather collar?" Her sister had somehow looked elegant in the simple silhouette of a dress with plumes, but Sam had no doubt that she'd end up looking more like a sick peahen. "Never mind. This'll do. I can't believe I gave away all my designer duds when I moved down here! What was I thinking?"

"That you wanted to start over. That you wanted to buy your own clothes, not wear the stuff designers sent just to hear their names mentioned at award shows. That you..."

Serena cut off her litany and Sam wasn't sure she was thankful or not. She missed her sister. Free-spirited and open-minded, Serena loved her uncondi-tionally—even after Samantha had schemed and ma-nipulated and downright lied in order to make Serena and Brandon see how they were meant for each other. Of course, she'd been right.

But even before then, Serena had always given Sam advice honestly and from the heart, whether she was talking about clothing or matters more personal. Like whether or not to pursue Dominick LaRocca, which they hadn't yet had a chance to discuss.

Brandon, her brother-in-law, suddenly comman-deered the cell phone. "What trouble are you getting me into now, Samantha?"

She huffed loudly. "Why don't you come home from your honeymoon and find out? You do have a business to run. And in less than an hour, you're going to have your first client."

"So I heard. Care to fill me in on the details? You aren't licensed yet..."

"Yeah, yeah. I know. He knows. I was completely up front with him. He's willing to take a chance on me since I saved him this morning from that rather scary crowd."

Brandon chuckled, having heard the tale by eavesdropping on her account to Serena. "I guess you were right when you claimed you had the instincts for this line of work. Any questions?"

Oh, she had a million questions. How does one carry a weapon when nearly naked? How would she go about crowding close to a man who sparked her flame, without letting him in on her intimate secret desire?

"No," she said, exhaling all her fear. Whether he knew it or not, Brandon needed her to succeed—for the sake of the business. And she needed to succeed for the sake of her own self-worth. That and her bank account. And his. "I don't think protecting Nick will be a problem. It's only two days, and Nick's assistant and I have worked out his schedule very carefully. I've even arranged backup in two locations with that friend of mine I told you about, the ex-cop. She's even going to watch the animals while I'm at the hotel."

"Good. You've got to know when to ask for help. Call me if you need anything. I guess we could head home…"

His voice died away, but by the sound of the pleasured groans that replaced it, Sam knew she couldn't ask him to cut short his honeymoon, even if they were four weeks overdue in returning to New Orleans.

"Have fun," she insisted. "Come home when you feel like it. I seem to have everything under control."

She disconnected the call and unknotted the sash of the robe she'd stolen from Serena's closet after her quick shower. Serena's long-haired Himalayan cat lit onto the bed beside the suit, scaring Sam with her quick, unexpected appearance.

"Damn, cat. Can't you wiggle your nose or something before you do that, Tabitha?"

Tabitha II's wide blue irises reflected complete indifference to Sam's scolding tone. Despite her aversion to animals of the feline persuasion, Sam reached out and scratched the cat beneath her chin and was rewarded with a loud, rumbling purr. The trill surprisingly calmed her nerves.

She had less than an hour to dress and meet Dominick and Anita at the hotel. Soon, she'd make her first official appearance at Nick's side as the woman who had saved him from bodily harm and then supposedly captured his heart. Only the three of them would know that the pairing was purely professional. The rest of the world would speculate and gossip about every look they exchanged, every touch they shared. She had no chance of keeping her identity secret—particularly not in New Orleans where her famous mother lived and practiced her psychic skills. Sam had no choice but to play the role of Nick's new lover to the hilt.

She tossed the robe aside and headed for the dresser where Serena kept her lingerie.

"What the hell, Tab, right? If I'm playing the girlfriend, I'd better make it real. Maybe he'll give me a bonus."

And for the briefest instant, Sam wasn't thinking about cash.

NICK SHOOK his last hand at precisely five o'clock. For two hours, he had mingled through a crowd of carefully screened convention attendees, each having passed through the tight security perimeter that Samantha, Anita and Tim had efficiently arranged. He'd then given his presentation on the new products La-Rocca would be introducing in the next year, stilling any unnecessary applause at the end by timing the dozen waitresses Anita had hired to appear just as he spoke his last sentence. Dressed in tuxedos and wide, friendly smiles, they handed out samples and small glasses of wine so that his listeners' hands and mouths were full and occupied with his food and drink.

He didn't want applause. He wanted increased sales. More shelf space in the stores. Better placement on endcaps and in Sunday advertisements.

Oh, and he also wanted Samantha Deveaux in his bed, but that was another matter entirely.

While the crowd savored and sipped, he glanced over his shoulder where Samantha sat on the dais beside Anita. She bent close to his cousin as if they were sharing some secret, but her gaze—alert and on guard—was trained on him. This time, he stared back. Starting at her feet, he worked his gaze upward, looking his fill while he kept his expression stoic. He didn't feel stoic, but he'd practiced the look so often he could call on his nonchalance even under the toughest circumstances.

Like when he was attempting to keep his arousal to himself.

Samantha dressed the part of sensual siren as if she was born for the role. Dainty heels, not high but strappy enough to be incredibly sexy, hugged her feet and launched his gaze slowly up incredibly toned, sinfully sculpted legs to that incredible skirt. The one that scarcely covered her thighs. The one he could make love to her in by barely lifting the material.

He turned aside to shake hands with another business associate before he had time to assess the snugness of her top. Had she dressed like that to play her part, or was she purposefully trying to torture him? Or both?

She slid behind him and slipped her hand beneath his jacket, settling her palm on his back with a simmering, electric crackle.

He winced, but hardly moved, becoming accustomed to her high-voltage touch. Now, if he could just adapt his intimate responses to her touch so easily.

"Ready to go?" she purred.

Nick eyed the crowd then glanced at his watch. At the moment, he'd spoken to all the people who needed speaking to, shaken hands with the power brokers who needed to be acknowledged. He had a dinner meeting scheduled in less than an hour at a French Quarter restaurant called Irene's, one Sam had claimed was well known among the locals and small enough for her to keep him out of harm's way. While he actually looked forward to sampling the award-winning cuisine and discussing business with the Japanese food broker who'd invited him, he didn't much anticipate the gauntlet they'd have to walk first.

"Are the television cameras out front?" he asked.

Samantha's smile was pure devotion, but her eyes betrayed, for an instant, the drama behind her expression.

"Oh, yeah. Two local news stations. One's an affiliate for *Entertainment Tonight* and the other shares a network with WGN. By the eleven o'clock news, your once-single marital status will undoubtedly be in question."

"WGN, huh? There's a Cubs game tonight. Won't my grandmothers be surprised if they break in with a news flash?"

A tiny frown formed on her plum-painted lips. At least it wasn't a pucker or purse. If she did that, he'd kiss her for sure.

"Are you certain you want to go through with this? Lie to your grandmothers, I mean."

Nick did feel an inkling of guilt over that part of the plan. But what was the cliché? *Turnabout is fair play?* Loving and well-intentioned though they probably thought themselves to be, his Nanas deserved a taste of their own pasta sauce after deceiving him about the label.

Besides, they really weren't the focus of his hoax. He was more concerned with the press and marriage-minded crazies—like the women disguised as nuns who'd staked out the lobby of his hotel earlier. If not for Samantha's efficient planning with Hyatt security, he would have been rushed once again before they'd arrived at the Expo for a second try at his presentation.

Nick shivered. Rushed by a half-dozen women wearing habits and *nothing* else. The image of them disrobing, wimples and habits flying, promised to give him nightmares for years to come.

"My grandmothers deserve to be a little misled. Once all this hoopla settles down, I might be able to talk some sense into them. Particularly if I can swing that European distribution deal in the meantime."

Sam nodded. He'd filled her in on his business goals during the car ride over. Discussing the details with her wasn't his preference, but he'd latched onto that conversation in hope of derailing his blatant stares and sensual speculation about what, if anything, she was wearing beneath her suit.

"Well, if swinging deals is your gig, we'd better get moving."

Sam made eye contact with a dark-haired security guard posted nearby, and then with Anita, who was remaining behind to field questions and supervise the booth. In an instant, a detail of guards appeared, ready to escort Nick and Sam to the exit where a mob of reporters awaited their first amorous appearance.

"That's very impressive," Nick complimented as he watched her coordinate their escape without saying a word or lifting a finger. "You make people move with just a look."

She was moving him too, though he hoped she didn't notice.

"Subtlety is always a useful tool in this business." She took his hand and coaxed him toward the security detail, her gaze flirtatious and her smile disarming.

Her tone and expression were seductive and brimming with heat, as if her whispered words were pillow talk rather than informational instructions. "There's a small group of women around the reporters, about fifteen at last count." She tapped her ear and he noticed she wore a tiny listening device, visible only because the wire was slightly lighter than her dark blond hair. "Two off-duty policemen are standing by at the car and two are positioned at the exit. I think we can make it outside with all our clothes intact.''

Nick nodded. Clothes while walking to the car were good. However, once they were alone in the back seat of the limo, he definitely had other ideas—ideas he'd most certainly have to keep to himself.

SAMANTHA FOUGHT THE URGE to bite her fingernails, which was weird since she'd never bitten her nails before. She was more likely to fidget when she was anxious. Luckily, walking at a fast pace eased her nervous energy. With each step she took, her thoughts cleared, focused on her goal.

Act the part. Be the bimbo. But as she, Nick and their security detail approached the bank of glass doors that led outside, the blinding gleam of television lights and the popping flashes from 35mm cameras threatened to wreck her resolve. She grabbed Nick's arm tighter and held her breath.

Both actions made her nearly dizzy. For a moment, she forgot who was protecting whom. A barrage of questions and comments fired as rapidly as the sharp clicks and screeching whirs that attacked from every imaginable angle. Sam fought flashbacks she thought she'd long since buried, memories from her high-profile past.

"Mr. LaRocca, is it true Ms. Deveaux saved your life?"

"Over here! Over here!"

"Have you finally found the woman of your dreams?"

"She's not really blond. You can tell she's not really blond!"

Now she remembered why she hated celebrity. Yet another reason why she'd left Hollywood.

"Ms. Deveaux, does he really look as good as the picture on the label?"

That one snapped Samantha back into character and forced her to focus on Nick. She could talk about Nick so long as she didn't have to talk about herself. She subtly pulled him to a halt beside her, her grin both sly and coy. Out of pure habit, she turned her face toward his, ruining a good shot of her but putting him in the center of the frame. She'd learned that trick from Anthony. Unfortunately, she'd also learned that some men would barter her and her privacy for the sake of publicity.

She blinked, wondering why she had so much trouble putting Nick into that category.

"That drawing on the label isn't nearly as impressive as the real thing. I should sue him for false advertising," she purred, leaning in close as if she intended to kiss him right there, but she turned back to the press at the last second. "But I won't, of course."

"Hey! Samantha! How does your mother feel about your new lover?" a female reporter asked, her tone genuinely interested, as if she was one of Endora's many devotees. "Does she predict marriage in your future?"

Samantha's stomach turned to leaden lava. She reminded herself that she'd suspected this would happen. But what else might they dig up? Something about her past? Her "youthful indiscretions," as her mother liked to call them?

Samantha shook her head, determined to deal with that potential disaster later. For now, she pulled a pat answer out of the practiced repertoire she thought she'd left behind on Sunset Boulevard.

"My mother is a strong believer in fate. I have no doubt she'll see my meeting Nick as exactly what it is."

A big fat lie.

"Mr. LaRocca, are you finally giving up bachelorhood?"

Sam watched Nick intently, for the sake of her act, of course, wondering if the nature of the question or the increasingly blinding lights caused the sudden, tense set of his shoulders. Either way, she sighed with relief, glad the reporters' attention shifted back on him. She tilted her head, attempting to scan the crowd and bright lights for danger. She glanced toward the limo, which was still a few more paces away than she would have liked. She started easing Nick toward escape with tiny side steps that resembled natural attempts to keep her balance in the surge of people.

Nick stopped their retreat by yanking Sam straight into his arms. She slammed against his chest—all muscle and rock-hard warmth. Rumbling reverberations echoed from deep within her, stealing her equilibrium and hampering her ability to think.

The instant his crushed-mint gaze met hers, the sounds of the media faded. Power emanated through his gaze, as if he owned a mute button on the entire world—and a play button right in her very center. He slid his hands to the small of her back. His fingers splayed over the curve of her backside, possessive, needful. Thrilling.

He lowered his face to hers and moistened his lips with a dart of his tongue. Samantha held her breath, nearly drowning in Nick's unique scent. Fine-milled soap. Spiced cologne. Aged wine. Man.

Oh, God. He was going to kiss her. Right here. Right now. In front of the entire world. And there wasn't a damn thing she could do about it. If she pulled away, she'd blow their cover. If she allowed him this intimate touching of lips, she'd detonate her tentative control over her libido.

At the last moment, Nick turned to face the cameras, allowing her the instant she needed to grasp and hold on tight to the fact that this was all an act. A ruse to fool the press. A scheme to thwart his grandmothers.

Unfortunately, the little details didn't erase the overwhelming truth—that she wanted Nick LaRocca with every fiber of her womanhood and every taut thread of her most secret desires.

"Bachelorhood is highly overrated," Nick said to the reporter, then turned his attention back to her. Again, the world around her seemed to freeze-frame.

"Don't you think?" he finished.

Sam knew his aside was meant for the press, so she didn't attempt a response. Truth was, she couldn't think to save her life. Or his. As his mouth neared hers, all she could do was close her eyes and welcome the sensations.

His mouth hot and urgent. Her surrender sweet and willing. Tongues twirled, briefly, as the camera flashes captured the moment for the whole world to see.

The minute he broke away, Sam instinctively pulled him closer to the car, hoping to look like the anxious lover she could never allow herself to be. Questions and shouts, and sounds Sam finally registered as jealous boos and hisses spurred her to hurry. Their lover act forced her to enter the limousine first, but with her security friend, Ruby, behind her holding tight to the door handle, Sam knew Nick would be right behind her.

He jumped in, his face immediately hidden by shadows. As the driver eased away from the curb, Nick leaned back into the plush leather seat across from her. A shaft of light from a street lamp streaked inside the car but revealed nothing in his expression.

He crossed his arms over his chest. Arms that had just held her close. Arms that under any other circumstance, she might have broken for embracing her so tightly—tightly enough to crumble the wall she'd built around her heart.

"I should have warned you," he said finally, his voice low and intimate, "about the kiss."

His words didn't actually form an apology, but then, they didn't really need to. They had a deal. She'd agreed to sacrifice her personal space to play the part of his lover.

So how come she felt as if she'd forfeited so much more?

She shook her head, then remembered not to be too emphatic in her denials. It was a dead giveaway. Casually, she plucked a tendril from behind her ear and twisted the curl around her finger.

"The kiss—"

What? Didn't mean anything? Hadn't affected her? Was simply part of their arrangement? Even she couldn't tell that large of a lie.

"—that's not what freaked me out. I'm sorry. I wasn't being a very good bodyguard, was I?"

Nick wore his confusion plainly and slid across to sit beside her. "What are you talking about? You planned that whole escape. Maybe you didn't notice, but your friend Ruby was right beside us the whole time."

Sam pursed her lips. No, she hadn't noticed, not until just before they'd gotten into the car. She'd been too taken aback by the cameras, the flashes, the questions about her mother.

Nick.

"Don't do that."

His whispered command, throaty yet pleading, snapped her gaze to his. The streetlights and shadows played across his rugged face, making his expression hard to read, but highlighting his expressive eyes. She saw a clear warning in the dark green irises. An omen most sensual.

"Don't do what?" she asked.

The darkness masked his touch, so she felt his fingertip on her lips before she registered that he'd lifted his hand. He traced along the bottom of her mouth, awakening the tingle from his kiss outside the Superdome, renewing the swirl of awareness spawned deep in her center. Tendrils of pure need pulled her nipples taut, then slipped into her lungs and captured her breath.

"You purse your lips when you're thinking," he said.

She swallowed. "I do?"

"It drives me crazy."

"It does?"

She watched the bob of his Adam's apple as the car pulled to a stop outside the bright lights of Harrah's Casino on their way to the French Quarter. Was his mouth watering the way hers was? She forced herself to focus on the riot of neon outside rather than on the intense, unguarded look on Nick's face. This time, the passion she saw there wasn't for the benefit of the press, but only for her. For them. Alone. In the back seat of a car more than roomy enough to accommodate a spontaneous response to their mutual desire.

Samantha scooted toward the door. She'd been that impulsive once, with Anthony, a man she'd hoped to someday love. They'd been so passionate for each other, so overwhelmingly connected, they'd never imagined his limo driver would install a camera to capture the intimate event and then sell the stills to a tabloid. But it had happened. Although Anthony Marks, sex symbol of the moment, had the clout, cash and attorneys to bury the pictures after the first print run, Sam had learned a hard lesson about fame, fortune and celebrity.

She'd lost something precious in the process. First, Anthony. Then her sense of privacy. But most of all, her faith in herself, in her ability to judge the difference between pure lust and potential love.

Like right now.

"Then I won't purse my lips anymore. I was just thinking about my mother."

As intended, her admission knocked the desire right out of his gaze. He returned to his seat across from her.

"Your mother, the psychic?"

Sam relaxed as the pull between them slackened. She'd thank her mother later for having such a dependable and well-timed effect. "My mother is more than just a psychic around here. New Orleans takes its supernatural history seriously. Madame Endora LaCroix Deveaux is not just a celebrity soothsayer, she's an icon. Government officials consult her. The police use her regularly to solve tough cases. Movie stars and dignitaries don't leave town until they've had their audience."

Nick nodded, but in the darkness, Sam couldn't gauge if Nick was as impressed as most people. But listening to herself, she realized she wasn't so doubtful of her mother anymore. All the things she'd said about Endora were true. Here Sam had her own personal conduit to the unknown, and she spent most of her limited time with her mother playing the skeptic. Pretending her Hollywood worldliness somehow saw through Endora's lame excuse for breaking up their family.

"If she's so accurate," Nick said, his tone confidant, "she'll know what our relationship is. Or do you think our stunt will upset her?"

Sam shook her head. She wasn't worried about her mother being upset, per se. She'd been upsetting her mother on a daily basis since she was five and begged to go live with their father in California only two months after he'd left the family to pursue his dream. Endora hadn't understood why a five-year-old would want to leave her own mother. She hadn't understood how Sam's child's heart had ached for the man who promised her wild adventures around the world, boundless excitement and limitless fun. Besides, Daddy had needed someone to take care of him. Mother no longer wanted the job. Serena was two years older, but Sam's sister wouldn't have left New Orleans even if the Mississippi had surged and drowned the city.

Disappointing her mother yet again wasn't her concern. But the added media attention on her because of her mother's renown—that had her squirming.

"We'll get a lot of local press, that's all. Because of Mother. Her phone is probably ringing off the hook right now."

"And this is a bad thing...why?"

"I don't enjoy living under a microscope, Nick. Been there, done that."

"With your father?"

Sam rolled her lips inward, smearing what was left of her lipstick and not caring. She'd told Nick she wouldn't share too much about her life, but since the reporters would more than likely dredge up her past with Anthony anyway, she figured she might as well tell him herself first. He needed to know. Should know. The truth might put a permanent damper on this burgeoning, wonderfully invigorating attraction.

"Devlin protected me from the press when I was a child. Which is why I had bodyguards. But when I got older and started doing stunts..." she smirked. "The novelty was too much for the tabloids to ignore. Then, about two years ago, I started dating Anthony Marks."

"Anthony Marks? Anthony...Marks, huh?"

Sam chuckled. Nick was so out of touch with Hollywood, the name meant nothing to him.

"Oh, wait. Wasn't he in that space movie? The astronaut who never wore a shirt?"

"He's the one." *Space Race* hadn't made much at the box office, but Anthony's shirtless scenes instantly made him a star. "So, you saw the movie?"

Nick frowned. "I haven't seen a movie since college. My niece has his picture hanging in her room. He's quite the heartthrob, I understand. No wonder you don't like the spotlight."

You don't know the half of it.

"But, I can handle it for a few days. It's what I agreed to. And I'm a woman of my word."

Nick left it at that. He whipped out his cell phone and called Anita while Sam gazed absently out the window. Landmarks blurred past—Jax Brewery. The Moonwalk. Street performers and vendors hawking dreams on Jackson Square.

As they waited to turn onto a side street, Sam realized that her affair with Anthony seemed a hundred years ago, when really, less than a year had passed since she walked out. While the relationship had ended at that moment, just after the incident with the photographs, she realized what she and Anthony had shared had never been a real relationship at all.

That had always been her biggest problem. She'd once again injected more into her affair with Anthony than had existed, and once again ended up disappointed and hurt. If only she'd seen their time together for what it was—a brief, fairly enjoyable fling—she might not have had so many wounds to lick when she returned to New Orleans.

And she might not be so reluctant to explore the attraction she shared with Nick, client or not.

Thanks to light traffic, they arrived at the restaurant quickly. Samantha had been careful to guard the location of Nick's dinner from the press, out of respect for the business associate who'd invited him. The small crowd gathered in front of the popular eatery seemed more impressed with the menus they read and the drinks they nursed than with anyone arriving in one of the many black stretch limos tooling around the city on a Friday night.

After they parked, Samantha slid across the seat toward the door. Nick stopped her before she could flip the handle.

"Wait, Samantha." He disconnected the call and pocketed the phone. "I don't want you to..."

Huffing with impatience, she impaled him with her best glare. She didn't want his sympathy, for God's sake, or his genuine concern. She couldn't battle them and her insatiable desire to make love to him all at the same time.

"Please. Don't. Don't play nice and all concerned about my feelings. I'm not your problem. I'm being so unprofessional here I'm surprised you haven't fired me on the spot. I'll deal with the consequences of my actions. Don't worry about me."

Nick chuckled, and as much as she tried to ignore the sensation, the rich sound rumbled through her like retreating thunder. As if the danger was over. As if the storm would soon subside. She knew better. She knew because Nick LaRocca turned her on and Sam was never one to deny her passions. Not even when danger stared her straight in the eye.

"A man would be a fool to worry about you, Samantha. I've never met a more capable, more in-control woman in my entire life. And that's including my formidable grandmothers."

Samantha smiled, grateful when the driver came around and opened the door. If Nick wanted to buy into the persona she so carefully exuded, then so be it.

Capable? Oh, yeah. She was capable right now of sliding to his side of the limo and showing him a lot more than just her pursed lips. In control? Barely. Only by clenching her hands into fists beneath her thighs was she keeping them to herself.

But his total confidence in her cool command of her emotions would play to her benefit. In the long run. But not now. Now, she was shaking. Shaking with frustration and recrimination and regret. Not because Nick had kissed her for the whole world to see, but because she couldn't ask for a private repeat performance.

DINNER WAS AS delicious as it was uneventful. Their Japanese host had married an exuberant British woman who entertained them all with fascinating stories and lively chitchat—and didn't seem the least bit concerned with who Samantha was, who'd she'd been, or if she and Nick were currently lovers. Sam spent the evening grinning, nodding and covertly watching for potential interlopers or reporters. Since they weren't spotted by anyone who knew Nick or by anyone who cared that he could offer a wife a weekly allowance worth more than the annual education budget of New Orleans Parish, Sam mostly sat back and tortured herself in silence.

Against her better judgment, if she had any judgment left at all after his mind-shattering kiss at the Dome, she watched Nick intently all evening. She watched how he savored his food, eating slowly, testing textures and inhaling aromas with each and every bite. She grew fascinated with the slow undulation of his mouth, the smooth way he retrieved his wineglass and sipped, all the time listening with intense interest to Mr. Ishimi and his wife—as if they were the only people in the room.

But that wasn't entirely accurate. Not once did he make her think he'd forgotten that she was sitting across from him. He didn't miss a single opportunity to suggest a choice from the menu, ask about the quality of her meal or inquire about her desire for anything else. His eye contact with her might have been brief while he focused on his official host, but the meeting of his gaze to hers was no less charged. Brevity made the looks intimate. Subtlety concentrated them with forbidden power. Had she any excess money in her bank account, she would have bet he was attempting to seduce her with his eyes.

Wager or not, he was succeeding.

After dropping his hosts at Le Pavillon Hotel, Nick quietly instructed the driver to return to the Hyatt. Though they'd discussed the night's accommodations that afternoon, Samantha now squirmed about the overnight bag she'd left in Nick's room. For the sake of

...yone who might be watching them and keeping score, she'd spend the next few nights on the Murphy bed in his businessman's suite. She'd packed the floppiest, most unappealing sleepwear she could pilfer from her sister's collection, but she couldn't help thinking about the sinful lingerie she'd impulsively worn beneath her suit.

Or how she so much preferred sleeping in the nude.

"I bet you can't wait to get to bed," Nick said, breaking the silence.

"Excuse me?" She might have had a wistful thought or two, but she felt quite certain she hadn't let her fantasy show.

"You look as tired as I feel," he clarified, chuckling at her assumption that he had implied something else. Obviously, he had not. "It's been a long day."

"Oh, yeah. Well...I don't need a lot of sleep. Four, five hours and I'm fine."

"Really? Me, too. Drives everyone I know crazy. I'm usually in bed by midnight and then I'm ready to go by 5:00 a.m."

Sam glanced at her watch. It was barely eleven o'clock. Just what would Nick do while she got into her jammies and prepared for what might very well be a sleepless night? Take a shower? Read his book? Order a nightcap and then attempt to seduce her?

Yeah. You wish.

"Is there anywhere you want to go first?" she asked. "Anyplace in New Orleans you wanted to see? Your schedule is pretty tight after tonight. Bourbon Street is probably just getting revved up. We could put in a very public appearance." Her suggestion sounded a bit more anxious than she'd intended, but the anticipation of being alone with Nick in his hotel room, with nothing to do and nothing to think about except the full breadth of her attraction, made her more than nervous.

When he didn't answer, she pursed her lips, trying to think of an alternative to partying in the French Quarter. He cleared his throat. For an instant, she didn't know what his chastising look referred to, until he drew his finger to his own mouth and tapped twice.

She rolled her lips inward and shrugged. "Sorry."

It was the last word spoken until they arrived at the hotel. They entered through the main lobby so anyone who cared would note that she was accompanying him to his room. The place was eerily quiet. Even the women who'd been stalking Nick for the past two days had apparently been drawn to the revelries across town.

"Ms. Deveaux!"

The hotel manager, waving a small, brown-paper-wrapped box, slipped away from the front desk just as they were about to enter the elevator.

Sam tensed, her instincts alert. She pushed Nick inside the elevator, but he slammed his palm against the side so the doors wouldn't close. She frowned impertinently, but his replying scowl won their brief contest of wills. Sam bit her tongue and waited for the manager to catch up.

"This came for you about an hour ago," he said, panting. "I waited past my shift to make sure you got it."

He grinned at Nick, who granted the eager manager the nod and smile he so obviously desired. Nick went for his wallet, but the manager shook his head. "Please, Mr. LaRocca. After the mix-up with room service this afternoon..."

Sam took the box and examined it. She had absolutely no experience with explosives, so she did what she saw actors do in the movies—she held it to her ear. When she did, she heard nothing ticking, but the distinct, blended scents of jasmine, magnolia and a rare Caribbean spice her mother used in her favorite tea tickled her nose. She turned the box over to see her mother's unique wax seal, an elaborate "E" in the center of a double-edged diamond.

"Thank you," she said to the manager, entering the elevator and tapping Nick on the elbow to release his hold on the door. Nick pressed the number to his floor.

"I take it nothing dangerous is inside."

Samantha gave the box a shake and could hear nothing recognizable. Her imagination instantly conjured an endless list of possible items her mother might find interesting to send along to her wayward daughter now that the news of her supposed love affair was all over the airwaves.

A gris-gris bag aimed at enhancing romance.

Dried and ground chicken claws to sprinkle around the bedside to ward off negative spirits.

Condoms?

Or worse, Grandmother Lizabeth's engagement ring, the elaborate ruby Endora had promised to Samantha since her third birthday.

"Dangerous? There's no telling," she answered. "It's from my mother."

"Open it," Nick encouraged, his humor perked by the chagrin Sam didn't bother to hide.

Samantha sniffed the box again and remembered that her mother had been collaborating with her sister, an aromatherapist, on a signature massage oil for Serena's spa. Serena's contribution, a unique blend of ingredients she kept secret from even her own sister, promised to enhance lovemaking. Endora's part, a charmed additive of unknown origins, would supposedly encourage commitment, even from the most reluctant lover.

She eyed him pointedly. "If your grandmothers sent you a box like this, out of the blue, after you'd just kissed someone on the late news, would you open it in front of me?"

7

NICK INHALED. He tried to make the action appear innocent as he slid the key card into the lock, but the sound of his quick intake of breath immediately drew Samantha's attention. She had to be the most observant woman he'd ever met. While he usually would have admired that trait, right now he was having a damn hard time hiding anything from her, least of all his elemental, inborn response to her standing so close.

Especially with that alluring scent emanating from the shaken box.

"Got a cold?" she asked, her tone just sassy enough to show she was well aware of his attempt to steal a whiff from the box.

"Actually, I *am* feeling quite warm."

"Maybe it's a fever." She eyed his forehead, but made no move to touch him.

Damn it.

"Maybe it's just New Orleans." *Maybe it's just you.* He swept his gaze over her once again, as he'd done so many times tonight, and this time he didn't bother to hide his interest. Why attempt the impossible? "This city gives a whole new definition to the word *hot*."

She slid around him when he pushed the door open. Her thigh briefly brushed against his leg, and though

PLAY HARLEQUIN'S

LUCKY HEARTS

GAME

AND YOU GET

- **FREE BOOKS!**
- **A FREE GIFT!**
- **YOURS TO KEEP!**

TURN THE PAGE AND DEAL YOURSELF IN...

Play **LUCKY HEARTS** for this...

*exciting **FREE** gift!*
This surprise mystery gift could be yours free

when you play **LUCKY HEARTS!**
...then continue your lucky streak
with a sweetheart of a deal!

1. Play Lucky Hearts as instructed on the opposite page.

2. Send back this card and you'll receive 2 brand-new Harlequin Temptation® novels. These books have a cover price of $3.99 each in the U.S. and $4.50 each in Canada, but they are yours to keep absolutely free.

3. There's no catch! You're under no obligation to buy anything. We charge nothing—ZERO—for your first shipment. And you don't have to make any minimum number of purchases—not even one!

4. The fact is thousands of readers enjoy receiving their books by mail from the Harlequin Reader Service®. They enjoy the convenience of home delivery...they like getting the best new novels at discount prices, BEFORE they're available in stores...and they love their *Heart to Heart* subscriber newsletter featuring author news, horoscopes, recipes, book reviews and much more!

5. We hope that after receiving your free books you'll want to remain a subscriber. But the choice is yours—to continue or cancel, any time at all! So why not take us up on our invitation, with no risk of any kind. You'll be glad you did!

© 1996 HARLEQUIN ENTERPRISES LTD. ® and ™ are trademarks owned by Harlequin Enterprises Ltd.

Visit us online at
www.eHarlequin.com

- **Exciting Harlequin® romance novels—FREE!**
- **Plus an exciting mystery gift—FREE!**
- **No cost! No obligation to buy!**

YES!

I have scratched off the silver card. Please send me the 2 FREE books and gift for which I qualify. I understand I am under no obligation to purchase any books, as explained on the back and on the opposite page.

With a coin, scratch off the silver card and check below to see what we have for you.

HARLEQUIN'S

LUCKY HEARTS GAME

342 HDL C6QH

142 HDL C6P7
(H-T-OS-06/01)

NAME   (PLEASE PRINT CLEARLY)

ADDRESS

APT.#   CITY

STATE/PROV.   ZIP/POSTAL CODE

Twenty-one gets you 2 free books, and a free mystery gift!

Twenty gets you 2 free books!

Nineteen gets you 1 free book!

Try Again!

Offer limited to one per household and not valid to current Harlequin Temptation® subscribers. All orders subject to approval.

The Harlequin Reader Service®—Here's how it works:

Accepting your 2 free books and gift places you under no obligation to buy anything. You may keep the books and gift and return the shipping statement marked "cancel." If you do not cancel, about a month later we'll send you 4 additional novels and bill you just $3.34 each in the U.S., or $3.80 each in Canada, plus 25¢ shipping & handling per book and applicable tax if any.* That's the complete price and — compared to cover prices of $3.99 each in the U.S. and $4.50 each in Canada — quite a bargain! You may cancel at any time, but if you choose to continue, every month we'll send you 4 more books, which you may either purchase at the discount price or return to us and cancel your subscription.

*Terms and prices subject to change without notice. Sales tax applicable in N.Y. Canadian residents will be charged applicable provincial taxes and GST.

BUSINESS REPLY MAIL
FIRST-CLASS MAIL   PERMIT NO. 717   BUFFALO, NY

POSTAGE WILL BE PAID BY ADDRESSEE

HARLEQUIN READER SERVICE
3010 WALDEN AVE
PO BOX 1867
BUFFALO NY 14240-9952

NO POSTAGE
NECESSARY
IF MAILED
IN THE
UNITED STATES

he didn't get a shock this time, the air crackled. His body thrummed.

"Luckily, your room is air-conditioned," she said oh-so-innocently. "The heat can make people do crazy things."

He followed her inside, and when she swung around to lock and bolt the door behind him, he had her trapped. God, she was gorgeous. She smelled like a freshly baked cinnamon creation steeping in a warm oven, injecting the air with a mouthwatering scent. He braced both hands on either side of her, waiting for her to turn around, waiting to find out if she tasted as sweet as she smelled.

Their first kiss had been too quick. He hadn't had enough time to recover from the jolt of pure desire to register all the flavors, or to savor the sensations.

And Nick was a savoring kind of guy.

"What kind of crazy things?" he asked, not really needing an example from her since he was clearly acting the part of the madman, despite the cool temperature in his suite. The aroma from the box was nothing compared to the fresh scent of her butterscotch hair, swept up in a loose twist, elegant in style, but erotically glamorous. He longed to kiss the soft curve of her exposed neck. Taste the extracts seasoning her skin.

"Like thinking you can trap your bodyguard this easily." Before he could react, she'd twisted and ducked out of his reach, darting into the room to turn on lights and check the closets and bathrooms for uninvited guests.

But she was not as immune to him as he'd thought this afternoon. The coy glances they'd exchanged at the restaurant, her instinctual reaction to his kiss at the Dome, the fire-hot tension simmering during the car ride back to the hotel told him all he needed to know. They may have made a deal to only act like lovers for the benefit of his grandmothers and the general public, but Nick hoped to sweeten the arrangement with some real interaction—for their personal enrichment alone.

"Everything all clear?" he asked, knowing he should bide his time. Samantha was now on the defensive. He needed her to relax. He needed to relax. He was wound so tight, he imagined he'd completely unravel if he didn't take things slowly.

And Dominick LaRocca didn't unravel. He was in control. Of his words. Of his actions. Of his desires.

Except now. Except when Samantha Deveaux was marching around his suite in a snug, sexy suit that did amazing things to her already amazing legs. He'd never experienced the brink of lustful insanity before. *Invigorating.*

"I need to check out your bedroom," she answered, marching toward the door with utter efficiency.

"Fine with me," he murmured as she swept by him.

She frowned before she entered the dark room, attempting to impale him with a sharp stare.

"Yeah, I figured."

Unfortunately for Samantha, her eyes were a little too dilated, her voice a little too breathless for her verbal swipe to cut his teasing mood.

He slapped his hand on his chest anyway, pretending to be offended. He liked this game they played. Amorous cat to saucy mouse. Besides, teasing her from a relatively safe distance tamped down his instinct to follow her inside his room to show her just how fine her presence in his bedroom could be. "What are you implying, Ms. Deveaux?"

She eyed him narrowly from the threshold, then gave up with a two-handed wave. "I'm implying that your arrogance is showing. Not every woman alive thinks you're some sort of gift to the feminine gender. Anita tried to warn me about you."

"Anita's been warning girls about me since I was ten and she was six," he said, shrugging out of his jacket and folding it over his arm. "And for the record, she was kidding then, too."

Samantha rolled her eyes and disappeared into his bedroom, leaving a trail of heat in her wake. Electricity wasn't the only fire she generated, but before he could complete one step in her direction to discover how hot a blaze they could stoke in his bed, she popped back out with a terse, "All clear."

"You barely checked," he accused.

"I checked enough. The door to the hall is still locked and bolted from the inside and there's no one hiding in your closet. So, here's the rule—you go to your room, I stay in here. I'll see you at 5:30 a.m."

"What if I want to work before I retire?" He gestured toward the work he'd left on the conference table in the center of what had just become *her* room.

She marched to his laptop and flipped down the top, then tidied the papers and files into one efficient stack.

"Aren't laptops an amazing invention? And the cell phone! Both so portable. They go everywhere, including bedrooms."

She leaned back on the table, causing the neckline of

her suit to gap just enough to give him a peek of a shiny purple satin strap. Then she pushed off his makeshift desk, slipping away before he had a chance to completely visualize the entirely different use for the smooth, flat table that had come to mind.

"Anita also told me you work too hard," she said. "And I'm sure she wasn't kidding about that. Why don't you forget about work tonight? You have a long day tomorrow."

He shook his head, trying to dispel the image of him luring Samantha onto the tabletop and forgetting all about work for more than just tonight. But there really was no use flirting with such a determined woman, especially when he wasn't sure where he wanted that flirting to lead. Okay, he knew where he *wanted* it to lead, he just wasn't sure that enticing his bodyguard into his bed was the best idea. For either of them.

He surrendered with a polite good-night, then went into the bedroom and closed the door behind him.

The bed, crisply turned down, with silver-wrapped candies on the pillows, immediately drew his attention. He peeled a mint and popped it into his mouth, hardly registering the cool, rich flavor on his tongue.

He could only taste Samantha, from a kiss that happened hours ago but still tortured him with hints of flavors and sensations utterly exotic and rare.

She thought he had a long day tomorrow? It would be nothing compared to the rest of the night.

SAM WAITED until she heard his door close with a resounding click. Then she breathed. The man was lethal! She slid into the leather chair, exhausted. Tempering her responses to his blatant sensuality sapped all her energy. He flirted with his eyes. He seduced with his words. When he'd trapped her against the door, his chest to her back, only an inch away from touching, from feeling his erection against her short-short skirt and the lacy panties she wore underneath... She forced herself to breathe again. They could have had sex right up against that door. Mind-shattering, borderline illicit lovemaking that would have knocked the double steel doors right off the hinges.

But she'd pushed away.

Fool.

When she heard the shower from his room turn on, she bolted into action. Now was the time for her to shower, when he was safely under his own stream of hot water and unable to accidentally walk in on her. She grabbed her overnight bag and her mother's box of surprises and tossed them into the guest bathroom while she tore off her suit and closed the door tightly behind her.

She stopped in front of the mirror and shook her head, removing the clips that held her hair in the sexy, slightly tousled chignon she knew made her look glamorous when she was honestly anything but. Hair down, loose and unbound, Samantha acknowledged that she was what she was—a woman with needs, simple desires.

But then, not so simple.

She traced the edge of her purple lace bra with her fingertips, watching, fascinated, as her nipples tightened and pushed her darker aureoles up from the low-cut cups. But she knew her touch wasn't responsible for the instantaneous physical reaction, the thrilling prickle of sexual desire shooting straight from her breasts to her belly and below.

Nick did this to her. Nick and his come-ons. Nick and his incredible but all-too-brief kiss. She was primed. Aroused. Charged as if they'd spent the past few hours engaged in foreplay.

Which in a sense they had.

She smoothed her hands down her rib cage and stomach, wondering why she worked so damn hard to keep slim and fit at the same time she worked so damn hard to prevent any man from sharing the fruits of her labor. She wondered if Nick liked his women thin and willowy, plump and soft, or like her, somewhere in the middle with a muscled edge from her hour of tae kwon do in the mornings, followed by her five-mile run, and then her weight workout every other afternoon. Her physical routine began years ago as training for the rigors of stunt work. She'd kept up the practice after quitting the business, first as a means to heal from her injuries, then to occupy her time. And, finally, to prepare for her new career as a bodyguard.

But there _were_ other payoffs she could explore. Other uses for her tight abs and slim thighs. Not to mention workouts for the parts of her body that didn't get nearly enough attention, that now resonated with the force of her heartbeat throbbing between her thighs.

If only she had the courage to walk across the hall.

A sound drew her to the door. A shout? Nick! Alarm dashed her desire along with her modesty, sending her scrambling out of the bathroom. She managed to think enough to grab her gun from her purse before she slipped into his bedroom, which was, *oh God*, completely dark.

NICK TURNED the shower on the hottest setting, watching the steam rise off the slick marble tile and coat the shower doors with a haze of hot moisture. In the grayness, he imagined a feminine silhouette—compact, yet curvy—emerging from the fog. Blond hair dampened to the color and texture of rich caramel. Eyes flashing like polished cobalt, dark and wide with desire.

Nick rolled his eyes and turned the faucet as icy cold as he could get during a New Orleans spring. He was losing his mind. It was pure insanity—caused by excessive testosterone and unrequited lust. He'd have to ask his doctor if such a diagnosis was medically possible. No, Nick realized as he tore off his clothes, he knew the ailment was possible. What he needed was a cure...and one that didn't include seducing Samantha Deveaux.

At least, not tonight.

Nick winced as he stepped beneath the surprisingly brisk shards of cold water, but by the time he'd soaped up and rinsed, his erection was no less pronounced and his brain was no less befuddled. Sure, Samantha was beautiful, in a sassy, what-do-I-care-if-my-hair-is-a-little-tousled sort of way. And her body, while not thin like Blair's or soft like Sophia's, seemed to find a happy medium in a toned fitness that she undoubtedly worked hard to maintain.

That's what confused him. Everything about Samantha was the opposite of what he'd believed for so long was his ideal woman. She was brash and opinionated.

She knew what she wanted and didn't need him or anyone else to tell her. She also knew quite clearly what she didn't want. Or at least, what she wouldn't allow herself to have. Nick didn't doubt that she was just as attracted to him as he was to her. He'd felt her instantaneous, unhindered response, quick though it was, to his kiss. She just had a much better handle on keeping her desires in check.

He adjusted the water temperature to a more comfortable warmth, then braced his hands on the shower wall and let the water sluice down his back. He closed his eyes, allowing the sensation to conjure the imagined feel of Samantha's hands trailing a similar path over his shoulders, down his spine, across his buttocks. The ache in his groin increased, but the feel of her touch, completely fantasized, was too delicious, too forbidden, to shake away.

It had been so long.

Too long between women. Too long since he'd even allowed himself the luxury of self-gratification to ease the sexual hunger he now fixated on Samantha. Under the circumstances, finding another woman to alleviate his lust was out of the question. He'd just have to take matters into his own hands. So he did.

"Don't," a female voice whispered, stopping his stroke. "Let me."

The bathroom light clicked off. A gentle glow from a scented candle flickered from the vanity. Nick couldn't believe this was happening. He'd never imagined Sam would come to him. Why would she? He had nothing to offer her but wild, lusty sex...and he felt certain that was way below her standard.

"Sam?"

"Shh." The shower door opened, then clicked closed behind a female form slightly smaller than Nick expected. The hairs on the back of his neck prickled over wet skin.

"Don't talk, Dominick. Let's just make love."

The minute she touched him, he knew. This wasn't Samantha.

"Who the hell—?"

The stranger grabbed him and began massaging. Roughly. He jumped back, nearly slipped, and banged his head against the showerhead. "Ow! Let go!"

"Come on, baby. Don't be shy. You know you want it. I've been waiting underneath your bed since this morning. She isn't going to give it to you. I'm willing. I'm here."

The bathroom light flashed on at the same time the shower door crashed open.

"Not for long. Let go of him and back off. Slowly."

With water stinging his eyes and a madwoman holding tight to his family jewels, Nick blinked, unsure if what he saw was real or some glimpse into his erotic fantasies. If this was a dream, he had definitely watched too many porno flicks in his youth. The sharp click as Samantha released the safety on her gun convinced him this was no triple X-rated film. The dark-haired stranger, more angry than guilty, released him and backed to the opposite side of the stall. The white satin teddy she wore clung wet to her skin, revealing cocoa-brown nipples on an ample bosom.

But she was nothing compared to Samantha. Blond hair wild and finger-combed. Nipples pouting from the edges of a sinfully sexy purple bra. Bare midriff. Plum panties that barely covered the sweet center of his torment. And the gun. Gleaming silver and cocked for business.

His best wet dream come to life.

The stranger thrust her fists on her hips. "What are you, the sex police?"

"No," Samantha answered calmly. "I'm just the bodyguard holding the gun. Come out of the shower." Sam gripped her pistol in one hand and motioned to the stranger with the other.

The woman shook her head and crossed her arms over her chest. "No way. I'm not going anywhere. Mr. LaRocca invited me here."

Nick opened his mouth to protest, but Samantha tossed him a towel and rolled her eyes, obviously in no need of an explanation. He shut off the running shower and covered up, pleased that Sam didn't believe the ridiculous lie.

"Is that so? Do you always call your lovers by their proper name? *Mr. LaRocca?* Unless he's a client and you're a..."

"I ain't no hooker. Mr. La...Dominick and me...we're going to be married."

Sam lowered her weapon and nodded for Nick to come out of the shower. He complied just in time for security to burst into his room, through the unlocked door he distinctly remembered was bolted before he'd gone into the bathroom. The first guard holstered his weapon as soon as Samantha flashed her gun. The second guard followed close behind, holding tight to a struggling young man wearing an ill-fitting room-service uniform and holding a camera.

Sam gave the woman an exaggerated frown. "Oh, looks like the banns won't be announced as planned. Unless you can arrange it from jail."

The first security guard grabbed a towel and wrapped up the intruding woman, then cuffed her behind her back.

"We caught this guy about to enter your room, Mr. LaRocca. The door was unlocked." When the guard, graying at the temples but obviously not blind, dared to eye Samantha while he detained their trespasser, she shifted her weapon a little higher. She lowered the gun when the man politely looked away.

With the situation now under control, Sam crossed her arms but made no other move to show that she was the least bit uncomfortable with the situation. "This is the young man who pretended to be from room service earlier, probably casing the place. Now he's got a camera and she's broken into Mr. LaRocca's room wearing next to nothing? Looks like a blackmail setup to me."

The woman and her camera-toting accomplice remained silent, but Nick agreed with Sam's assessment. Pictures of him engaged in a sordid tryst, setup or not, could be both valuable and damaging. Once again, Sam had saved him.

Nick cleared his throat. "Take these people out of here and call the police," he instructed.

"The NOPD will want a statement from us," Sam informed him.

The last thing he wanted to do tonight was talk to

cops. "We'll press charges and file a report in the morning. Not before."

Nick's tone elicited decisive nods from hotel security.

"And keep this quiet," Sam added. "I don't think your hotel or your manager would appreciate the bad press." She followed her implication with a quick little grin said, "Thank you and goodbye" in one brief flash.

They made a great team. By the time the room emptied and the door slammed shut behind him, Nick realized he was standing in the middle of his bathroom, holding a towel around his waist, dripping wet, and completely stunned by what had just happened.

Samantha was obviously no better off. She'd just broken up a possible assault on his very naked person. And in her underwear, too.

Incredibly sexy, sewn-for-seduction underwear.

She slid the gun onto the countertop and combed her fingers through her hair in a hard thrust. "God, Nick. I'm so sorry."

He slammed his lips together, suddenly aware that he was gaping, openmouthed, at the woman of his fantasies, nearly naked, packing heat and...apologizing?

"For?"

Rushing by him to lock the door from the inside, Samantha shook her head and plopped down on the bed. "I'm so not ready for this job. Brandon's going to kill me for screwing this up."

Nick's muddled brain snapped clear. *Woman in distress.* This he could do. He shrugged into the hotel-supplied robe, then grabbed a second one from the closet and wrapped it around her shoulders as he sat beside her on the bed.

"Samantha, you rescued me again. And just in time, too."

Sam shook her head, apparently not ready to hear his positive spin. "How'd she get in? I *know* that door was bolted from the inside. I checked when we got back."

Nick realized the rustling sound he'd heard that morning had *not* been the air conditioner or a figment of his imagination. "She said she hid under the bed since this morning."

"Under the bed? That I didn't check." Sam pulled the lapels of the robe closer as she noticed Nick's proximity. "That guy with the camera was the same one who brought up the wrong room-service order this afternoon. The chick in the teddy must have used the side hallway to break into the bedroom. The room-service ploy distracted me so I wouldn't hear."

Nick wasn't about to admit that he *had* heard something and his well-documented male pride hadn't allowed him to tell her. "That private hallway was supposed to have been locked before I arrived."

"She could have stolen a passkey with the waiter's uniform. Or picked the lock."

Sam's frown was repentant, and nearly as maddening as her most thoughtful pucker. "I guess I should have looked under the bed."

Her honest admission of her error grabbed him right in the middle of the chest. She might have checked under the bed had he told her that he'd heard something suspicious. But who screwed up when wasn't important now. He only wanted to remove the embarrassed look from her face.

"Who checks under a bed for a grown person?" he asked. "Besides, most hotels have those kickers on the bed frames so you don't lose your socks."

Sam's tiny grin warmed the chill the air-conditioner was wreaking on his wet skin. "You almost lost something more valuable than socks." She glanced down to the front of his barely closed robe. "That woman had a death grip on the future LaRocca progeny. Are you all right?"

Wanna check for yourself? Nick nearly let the invitation fly, but his instincts told him Sam's pride and confidence were still too wounded to deflect such an innuendo. "I'd rather not think about it. So, what? They planned to get me in some compromising position and then blackmail me into marriage?"

"Marriage...money. No telling. You know, she must have waited under that bed all afternoon until we left for the Dome and then hid again when we came back." Sam slipped off the side of the bed and ducked under the edge of the comforter to look under the bed. Big mistake. Her robe fell open just at the perfect angle to renew the throbbing in Nick's groin—the throbbing that had absolutely nothing to do with the physical assault on his person.

"She must have really wanted you," she said.

Her assessment sounded too much like a personal admission—too much like those hypothetical scenarios where someone talks about themselves in the third person—for Nick to let her comment go. He extended his hand to her, inviting her to stand when he did.

"I know what it feels like to want someone that badly," he said.

She licked her lips.

He thought he'd die.

"You do?" she asked.

He answered with a slow nod.

She pursed her mouth. Pink. Moist. His entire body tensed with the rigid need he wasn't sure he could contain much longer.

"I asked you not to do that," he whispered, reaching one finger to press on the center of her tightened lips.

She gently guided his hand to her cheek. "Because it turns you on?"

"Oh, yeah."

She smiled, then pressed a tiny kiss in the center of his palm. He sucked in a breath, sure she was torturing him, sure she was determined to drive him utterly insane.

"I can't seem to help myself," she answered. "I wonder why that is."

8

THE RINGING SOUND barely registered in Samantha's ears until Nick swore. She moved to grab the receiver, but he pulled her back into his personal space.

"Let it ring," he said.

She shook her head, half of her thankful for the interruption, half of her mad as hell. "It could be the police. If we don't answer, they'll come up and check on us."

With a growl, he tore away from her and snatched up the phone with a loud and curt, "What?"

His sudden absence hit her like an icy wind, throwing her off balance and weakening her knees. Luckily, the bed caught her when she sat to think. To regroup.

Good Lord. Had she just propositioned her client? The man she was supposed to protect? The man she'd just seen in all his nude and perfect glory, while she'd pranced to his rescue in underwear too racy even to be Victoria's best-kept secret?

Of course, if she'd done her job right, Nick wouldn't have needed rescuing. From their kiss at the Dome to the tension in the limo, she'd battled her overwhelming desire to make love with him. She'd hurried through her search of his bedroom earlier in hopes that a good night's sleep would unwind the tense coil of need he'd spun with his sexy banter and skilled kiss.

She *had* checked the closets and bathroom, as well as

behind the curtains and even inside the tall armoire. But the bed? Oh, no. She'd given that particular piece of furniture a wide berth. Certain his scent lingered on the sheets, she'd utilized every ounce of her control just to keep from burying her face in his pillow. Her brief glance at the bed had instantaneously hit her with an erotic flash-forward vision. Nick beneath her. Above her. Unclothed and carefree, rolling and laughing and discovering each other over, under and around the soft, feathery comforter.

Had she been able to control her overactive imagination, she might have found the woman hidden beneath the frame, waiting for Nick to get into bed or into the shower, anywhere vulnerable where she could trap him and fulfill her scheme.

Sam braced her elbows on her knees and buried her face in her hands. In all honesty, she didn't know if the woman was certifiable or brilliant beyond words.

Nick's voice coaxed her from her one-woman pity party.

"No, no. It's been a rough night. I didn't mean to bark." His tone calmed from frustrated to professional, but his impatience showed by the way he marched around the nightstand and knotted the phone cord while he spoke—she assumed from the conversation— to the hotel manager.

Sam watched him, amazed at the ease with which he caged his raw power. Unleashed, such energy would make the man a magnificent lover. She already knew from his actions at the restaurant that he was attentive, concerned with her needs. She also knew from watching him at the Expo that he preferred to be in charge. In careful control. To a woman like Samantha, a woman forced by her circumstances to take control even when she didn't want to, Nick's combination of intuition and strength was inherently seductive. Irresistible beyond her wildest dreams.

Sam twisted her fists into the downy comforter beneath her, and the gentle bounce of the mattress reminded her that she was very close to living that particular dream. Too close. She should get up. Get out. Book the first flight out of New Orleans and go back to the illusory world of Hollywood where she could convince herself that she was content with brief affairs and meaningless sensual interludes.

But she'd come home to New Orleans in search of something more. Roots. A home. People who liked her just because she was Samantha and not because she could get them a job with her father or bankroll their next film. So far, the best thing she'd found in New Orleans was Nick, a man whose obligations and goals would take him out of her life in two days.

But how could she ignore the act of fate that had thrust Nick and her together? Or deny the rush of attraction she hadn't felt in so very long? Sam had learned, from her father and every other Hollywood player she'd ever known, to seize opportunities before they slipped away.

Like right here. Right now.

"No, I'm sure we're not going to sleep anytime soon," Nick said into the receiver. His voice was matter-of-fact, but his eyes sought hers and practically glowed with endless possibilities—glittering sparks of sensual promise that caused an electric shiver to run from her fingers to her spine. The anticipation of a total erotic torrent made her light-headed, as if she was standing on the top of a ten-story building, preparing to jump, aiming for the safety mat inflated below.

"That's completely unnecessary. No...yes, of course. I appreciate your hospitality." Nick hung up the phone. "That was the hotel manager. He wanted us to know that the police arrived, and while they wanted to come up and take a report right now, he convinced them to wait until morning to investigate."

Samantha nodded.

"He's bringing up a nightcap for us, to help us sleep after our 'disturbing incident.'"

She nodded again. "*Disturbing* is a good word."

Tension coiled in Sam's belly, and as the sensation intensified, she bolted off the bed. This wasn't right. She wasn't supposed to be attracted to her client any more than she was supposed to be sitting on his bed dressed in nothing but sexy lingerie and a borrowed robe. Especially not with room service on their way up.

"I'd b-better get dressed," she stuttered, gesturing to the door that separated their rooms.

He shook his head. "Just relax, Sam. The manager is bringing it himself. I can answer the door."

"But it's my job."

Nick hesitated. His eyes narrowed, and this time *he* pursed his lips. She could see why he found her little habit so infuriating. His lips were inviting, full and de-fined, beneath an incredibly Grecian, incredibly regal nose. If she hadn't stopped herself, she would have puckered her own mouth in response.

"Then I'll finish my shower and join you in a few minutes," he said.

Sam smiled when Nick disappeared into the bathroom and shut the door tightly behind him. He still trusted her to do her job. Why, she had no idea. But his faith in her zapped the last of her regrets out of her head. She'd screwed up once—she wouldn't again. Not with her job. Not with her life.

Fortunately for her, she couldn't think of a single way that making love with Nick could be considered a mistake. Not if she proceeded with her eyes open and her expectations nil. Not if he still wanted her with the same overwhelming attraction she felt for him.

Anticipating the arrival of the hotel manager, Sam nearly changed into her floppy pajamas before realizing her robe and tousled hair would play perfectly into their still make-believe love affair. She chuckled to herself, imagining what the security guards had told the hotel manager about what they'd seen when they came to collect the trespasser and her intended accomplice.

Swear to God, boss. She was holding a 9mm in purple underwear.

She tossed any embarrassment aside. She still wasn't worse than the naked nuns.

That she'd carry a gun when on a date with her new lover would make sense since everyone knew she was employed with No Chances Protection and that she and Nick had met when she was working security at the Dome. An outrageous incident like a nearly naked woman attacking Nick in the shower only for him to be rescued by his scantily clad lover would undoubtedly make the morning talk shows and add nicely to the illusion she and Nick were creating.

Illusion. And she thought she'd left that all behind in Hollywood.

Perhaps she had.

The knock came quickly, and Sam answered the door after checking the peephole. The manager offered profuse apologies, which Sam accepted along with a cart laden with a bottle of cognac, a chilled magnum of Asti Spumante and two dishes covered with silver domes, one on ice and one warmed with Sterno. The manager informed her that he'd posted two guards at the elevator and he offered one for the door, but Sam insisted the third man was overkill.

There was such a thing as too close for comfort.

She rolled the cart into the living room, placing the peace offerings from hotel management on the low coffee table. Familiar aromas emanated from the heated bowl—butter and sugar and fresh, roasted pecans. She was just lifting the top when Nick came into the room, dressed again in his loosely sashed robe. His dark hair was combed and slicked back, making his features even more angular, his green eyes more piercing. Pajama pants, striped blue and white cotton, covered his knees and ankles and added warmth to his cool yet potent masculinity.

"That smells incredible," he said.

She took a long sniff. The action sent her spiraling back in time, to Miss Lily's kitchen in her mother's house. She'd been no more than four, begging to lick the spoon while Serena mixed the pecans they'd picked from the tree in the backyard with the melted butter and caramelized sugar Miss Lily had set to simmer in an old, battered pot. They'd drop the mixture onto rolls of butcher paper lining the countertops and listen to Miss Lily tell stories until the praline candies cooled enough to pilfer. They would wrap the rest in colored cellophane to share with the neighbors on All Hallows' Eve.

When Sam opened her eyes, Nick was standing directly across from her.

"Where were you?" he asked.

She smiled shyly. She rarely allowed herself the luxury of childhood memories, because a good one inevitably led her to a bad one, like her first Halloween away from New Orleans when her father had his maid take her trick-or-treating because he had a film to edit. Shaking her head, she plopped down on the sofa. "I was back in Miss Lily's kitchen."

"Miss Lily?"

"She's my mother's cook and very best friend in the universe."

Nick sat on the love seat next to the couch and examined the bottle of cognac. "A cook, huh?"

"The finest in all of New Orleans. You have no idea how much money she's been offered to open her own restaurant."

He set the dark brown bottle aside and lifted the wine out of the ice-packed bucket. He smiled and promptly began removing the foil and wire protecting the plastic cork. "New Orleans has an amazing culinary past. I'm ashamed I've never visited here before now."

Sam eyed the bathroom, wondering if she should excuse herself to shower. But the soft terry cloth of the robe felt lush and warm against her skin, a sensuous contrast to the soft chafe and subtle pinch of the purple lace. Despite their mutual state of undress, or maybe because of it, Samantha had no desire to leave.

"Can I pour you a glass of Asti? This is my favorite," he admitted, his grin somewhat boyish, as if he was sneaking a glass of alcohol during his parents' dinner party.

He showed her the label and she smiled. "That doesn't cost more than fifteen dollars in a grocery store."

"The best things aren't always the most expensive."

Samantha laughed, then slid a chilled, empty flute toward him. She silently agreed that the Italian sparkling wine was delicious, but that wasn't the reason why she wanted to share a glass with Nick. There was an innocent decadence about it, a forbidden indulgence that seemed entirely safer than what she really wanted to do—shed her own terry-cloth robe so she could climb into his. Blaming the heat from the Sterno for the jump in her body temperature, she patiently waited for Nick to pop the cork and pour them both some wine.

"What's hiding under the other cover?" Nick asked, handing her a fizzling glassful.

She retrieved the wine, then leaned forward to reveal a glistening bowl of red, ripe strawberries.

"Oh, my," she said. "You must tip well. This is some spread."

"Are you hungry?"

Sam swallowed a mouthful of wine, knowing full

well that a sip would be entirely more genteel and appropriate. But at the moment, she didn't care about propriety. Nick's voice was low and throaty. His dark lashes were lowered, shading his intense eyes just enough for her to know that he meant more than he said. His question brimmed with meaning beyond her appetite for food, and her answer had to match his, or she'd lose out on more than just a contest of wits.

Bubbles filled with courage trickled down her throat.

"I've been told I'm insatiable," she answered, plucking a berry from the bowl.

His expression didn't change.

"So have I. Maybe that's why I'm so good at what I do."

Sam stopped, smacking her lips closed before she took a bite. Okay, she was good at this tease thing, but he was better. Or they were at least evenly matched.

But he smiled when she did, and that knocked the tension down a peg. He was toying with her—and she with him. She shook her head while she took a bite of the large strawberry, closing her eyes as a burst of tart freshness filled her mouth. Nick was not only adept at the game of flirting, he made the interactions fun. Exciting. Charged and unpredictable.

Sam couldn't remember the last time she'd enjoyed such banter. She didn't know how he'd created the illusion, but she actually felt that, for once, she could let go and be herself and lose nothing in the process.

Couldn't be.

Impossible.

"What are we doing here, Nick?" she asked, not sure

she wanted an answer since it might destroy the oddly wonderful combination of seduction and camaraderie they'd somehow created.

"So far, we're sharing delicious wine and, soon, a tempting dessert."

"Is that all?"

He shrugged and took a long sip. "The night's young. I told you, I'm a night owl. A hungry night owl."

"So have a strawberry," she said, choosing a second fruit, but this time lingering over the steaming praline sauce, prolonging the act of coating the berry in the delectable concoction.

"Oh, I intend to," he said, tilting his glass toward her before he drew in another measured sip. "But ladies first."

Nick sat back when Sam dragged her strawberry through the praline sauce in slow, undulating streaks, seemingly oblivious to the sensual rhythm she wove. His trained palate conjured the combined tastes of the buttery, browned sugar sauce, the crunchy pecans, and the tart fruit—all before she took a single bite. Before he stole the tastes from her.

His mouth watered. When Samantha licked her lips, then drew the dripping berry closer and closer to her mouth until she finally took a single ravenous bite, his taste buds exploded.

He knew each flavor, each texture, by heart. He knew the nuances well enough to combine them in his brain. Yet, he craved one special essence, one elusive extract only Samantha could add to the mix. A secret ingredient. Alluring. Subtle. Elemental to the union of sweet and sour on the tongue. His tongue with hers.

She bit and chewed slowly, lowering her lashes to half-mast as the heavenly flavors danced on her every feature. "Good God, Nick. You've got to try this."

He took a hearty sip of his Asti Spumante, ignoring the rush of effervescence, then stole the few inches he needed to reach her mouth with his.

"I intend to."

She met his gaze boldly. A tiny, strawberry-stained smile told him she wouldn't protest, propelling his appetite from hungry to ravenous—all for a taste of her.

Her mouth was softer, riper, than the fruit. Her tongue inherently sweeter. She smelled of pralines and perfume. Felt like velvet warmed by a fire. He'd intended to take only the briefest taste of her, but Sam moaned and grabbed the lapels on his robe. He couldn't back away.

But he had to give her one last chance. One final opportunity to stop the momentum.

But first, he finished kissing her. Thoroughly. Until he knew every contour of her mouth, every slick groove in her teeth, every pleasure spot on her tongue and lips.

"I can't believe we just kissed again," Samantha said, making absolutely no move to back away. Nick searched her eyes for any hint of regret, any inkling of anger at him or at herself.

He saw only pleasure. Intense desire.

"Fantasies do come true, I guess. I, for one, am damn glad," he said.

"But what are we doing? Living for the moment and

enjoying each other—or believing our own press and taking our fake affair way too far?"

Nick respected every reason she had to question his timing. Their timing. Their motivations. They'd known each other for less than a day, and in that time, he'd shown her only slightly more than his established persona—the Nick even his family thought was the real him. The facade bought him a certain degree of separation, allowing him to operate as he needed to as CEO of the family business. He wore his confidence to the point of arrogance. He feigned flippancy to the emotions that drove a woman's heart.

But Sam's heart? From what he could tell, she protected her heart with all the vigilance of a seasoned bodyguard. She was a painfully private woman in an increasingly public world.

They were so alike, Nick steeled himself against a tremor of pure need.

"I won't be just some conquest...some shot to your ego," she insisted.

He smoothed his hands up and down her arms, hoping to disguise his own intense reaction to her honesty. He succeeded only in eliciting a soft purr from the back of her throat, the vibrations of which seeped straight into his skin. "A nearly naked woman hiding under my bed and accosting me in the shower is enough to last any man's ego for a lifetime."

Sam smirked and, on her, the wry smile looked remarkably sweet, especially so close up. They'd yet to pull away after their kiss and spoke nose to nose, like the intimate lovers they could be.

"Then we're just living for the moment? Enjoying what we have, here and now?"

Nick surrendered to the liquid blue of her irises and touched a kiss just above each eyebrow. Her lashes fluttered, tickling his chin.

"Sounds too good to be true," Nick confessed. "I can't remember the last time I've been with a woman who doesn't seem to *need* anything from me."

"You're so wrong, Nick."

"You don't need my money," he reasoned. Until this moment, he never would have described himself as jaded or disillusioned with women. He'd always viewed his doubting attitude as a practical, logical deduction based on a woman's ulterior motives.

But with Samantha, he didn't care what her ulterior motives were. In fact, he seriously doubted she had any. But if she had them, he suspected he'd willingly provide whatever she wanted just for the chance to slip inside her giving warmth.

"I do need your money," she protested. "I need this job. I told you that from the start."

He brushed his lips over her bangs, inhaling the spicy scent of her shampoo. "You could find something else in a heartbeat. You may need this job, but not enough to sleep with me to keep it."

She glanced down, shaking her head as she laughed lightly. "Then why should I sleep with you?"

Nick smoothed his palms along her cheeks, weaving his fingers into her fragrant hair, tilting her gaze to meet his. "Because I'm offering you one night, just for us." He pressed his lips against her soft cheek, just below where his thumbs caressed her skin. "A man." He kissed her chin, skipped her mouth, and placed a tender peck on the tip of her nose. "A woman." His hands trailed down her neck, dipping into the open collar of her robe. "An insatiable hunger."

Samantha's bold stare never left his. The dilation of her pupils and the slight rasp in her breathing were the only outward signs that she'd even heard his proposal. An expert negotiator, he appealed to what he knew she wanted most.

"No strings, Samantha. No expectations. An utterly discreet and private night for us alone."

Her gaze narrowed as she slipped her hands between them to work the knot on his robe. "You've left out the most important detail, Nick."

He straightened, wondering what he could possibly offer her that he hadn't already voiced. But the glint in her sapphire gaze told him she was toying with him again, manipulating him with the same skill that she used to release the tie on his robe and toss the terry cloth aside.

She nuzzled close, grazing her lips over his bare chest. Instantly, he knew exactly what sensual item he'd inadvertently forgotten to mention.

"Oh, you mean the part where I promise to make all your erotic fantasies come true?"

She stood so close, he felt the thrill shimmy up her spine and light her eyes with hot fire.

"I didn't forget, Samantha. There are just certain things that go without saying."

9

WITH A SINGLE GLANCE and a brief caress, a wealth of knowledge passed between them.

That she could trust him.

That the passion surging between them was natural and honest and undeniable.

That she was going to nourish his erotic fantasies at the same time he satisfied hers. And she knew *exactly* how.

She lifted herself on the balls of her feet and placed a brush of a kiss along the base of his chin, where a tiny, almost unnoticeable cleft hid beneath his incredible lips. She had one particular fantasy in mind that craved immediate attention, if for no other reason than to erase the picture of another woman accosting him in the shower.

"I'm feeling a little grimy after our long day." She whispered her confession directly into his ear.

"I should have invited you to share my shower."

She chuckled and shook her head, sliding her palm from his cheek to his chest, then across to his shoulder and down, where she clutched his hand in hers.

"Your shower was a little too crowded," she said, winking.

He rewarded her quip with a reluctant grin. "You're very funny, you know that?"

She wiggled her eyebrows, and he pulled her closer. He kicked his robe away and tried to grab the sash on hers, but she deflected the move with a skillful twist. She wanted Nick. She wanted to be naked with Nick. But the promise of a slow, deliberate seduction, the anticipation of a long-awaited payoff of the most sensual kind, outweighed both their needs to act quickly. Making love with him—tonight, with no promises, no commitments between them—filled her quota for spontaneity.

The rest would be planned and executed with her trademark precision.

Like the bathroom in Nick's half of the suite, hers also had candles on the dresser which she lit while he watched from the doorway. As soon as the fourth and final wick flared, Nick flipped the light switch, bathing the bathroom in a flickering kaleidoscope of warm light. The candles, doubled in intensity by their reflection in the mirror, were unscented, but as the flames warmed the intimate space around the vanity, Samantha smelled the unique fragrance seeping from her mother's brown paper box.

She slid the parcel closer to her as Nick entered the bathroom, shutting and locking the door behind him.

"I can't believe you haven't opened that yet. Aren't you curious?"

Sam fingered the taped edges. Whatever was leaking from inside had now darkened the paper from tan to chocolate. The substance was oily and slick on her skin. Nick came up behind her, examining the package from over her shoulder.

"What's that?"

Sam drew her hand to her nose, rubbing her fingers together as she inhaled the unusual mixture of scents. "Some kind of oil," she answered, and with each word, her fingers grew instantly hot. Her eyes widened. Possibilities most erotic scrambled her ability to speak any further.

"The aroma is so enticing, so—"

Sam turned around and smeared some of the oil across Nick's lips, silencing him. "The aroma is nothing compared to this."

She blew a soft breath on his mouth. The instant the heat flared on his lips was reflected in his eyes. He cooled the sensation with his tongue, and his grin, while narrow, spread effectively across his face.

"It's flavored and it reacts to air by getting hot? I think I'm going to like your mother."

Samantha turned around and unwrapped the box. "Thank my sister. I bet she and Brandon had a great time testing this."

Inside the box, Samantha found a small, antique glass vial of the potent mixture sealed with wax that had somehow cracked just enough to release the undeniable fragrance into the air—enough to spill some of the magic elixir and pique Sam's undeniable curiosity. Sam had no doubt that her mother sent the oil to somehow manipulate her or her present situation, but with Nick standing behind her, nuzzling her neck while his fingers deftly undid the sash on her robe, she didn't care. She took the bottle from the box and popped off the wax seal and tiny cork, both tied with twine made of natural hemp.

Dangling from the string was a pair of foil squares, and her grandmother's exquisite ruby ring.

Two out of three isn't bad, Sam recalled her guess about the box's contents. She plucked the condoms free, realizing they actually had more than two, and handed them to Nick. She hid the ring behind the artful fan of face towels the maid had crafted on the vanity. Despite her mother's cunning intentions, tonight wasn't about commitments or marriage or happily-ever-anythings.

Pleasure was their primary goal. Discovery and adventure and living for the moment, relishing sensations, focusing on nothing but this one erotic interlude—to milk the experience for every last drop of pure excitement.

Kind of like jumping off a building. Or driving a car rigged to explode when the wire is tripped.

Or jumping into a fray of frenzied females to rescue a man that could, with a single, intimate touch, rescue her right back.

Sam swung around just as Nick snapped the sash out of the loops. He worked the robe off her with no resistance, his eyes alight at the revelation of her wicked purple bra and panties.

He perused her with brazen approval. "You didn't tell me your family dabbles in sex aids," Nick teased, tapping the slippery bottle she held.

Sam grinned, drawing tiny circles around the rim with the tip of her finger.

"With a little imagination, your pasta sauce could be a delicious sex aid."

As the possibility played in his mind, his tongue

darted out to moisten his lips. "Have I told you that I like the way your mind works?"

He didn't have to tell her. Judging by the lascivious images popping into her brain with each and every glimpse she caught of his magnificent chest and shoulders, they were operating on exactly the same wavelength. "Have I told you that I like the way your body works?"

"You haven't seen my body work. Not yet."

She tilted one eyebrow as she glanced past him at the shower stall.

"That doesn't count," he insisted, obviously remembering that she'd seen him in the nude when she came to his aid in the shower.

"Sure it does." Sam tapped a small puddle of oil into her palm. "I may have only gotten a brief glimpse, but that's all I needed for inspiration."

She rubbed her hands together and moved to smear the slickness on him, but he caught her by the wrists to stop her assault. "I got more than a brief glimpse of you, Samantha. And you've been inspiring some incredibly sinful thoughts since we first met. Before I ever knew that you favored purple lingerie."

"What? When I tackled you and got you out of the crowd?"

Nick chuckled as he slowly turned her around, wrapping both her wrists in one big hand, so that when she faced the mirror, he could retrieve the other hand and control when she applied the oil. And where.

"Just a bit later," he replied. "When I tackled you against the door."

"That was just the static electricity," she claimed, inhaling sharply when Nick used his teeth to slide down the straps on her bra so they dangled off her shoulders. The demicups loosened and gapped, barely covering her aroused nipples.

"Maybe." Nick pressed his body completely against hers. His erection strained through his light cotton pajama pants, full and hard and long. "But let's see if we can't generate something a bit stronger."

He forced her hands together.

"Close your eyes," he whispered.

She watched his reflection in the mirror, intrigued by the shadows playing across his muscled shoulders, captured by the light flickering in his fathomless, dark green eyes. He dipped his head to deliver his next instruction on a warm breath directed into the shell of her ear.

"Trust me."

She let her lids drop. His strong, thick fingers and wide palms completely covered hers, holding them clasped together. The sensuous slide of the oil in her palms created desires more dangerous than any stunt she'd ever performed, stoking needs no lover to date had ever dared to satisfy.

The infused aromas of the massage oil intensified as her hands warmed the mixture at his command. Floral essences, sweet and exotic, battled with that elusive spice that had no name, but that she'd known her entire life. The scent of comfort. Hot tea on rainy days. Scented flames on sad nights. Soon the aromas meshed with Dominick's natural musk, already heightened and strengthened by a woodsy shampoo. Sam breathed in deeply, allowing the sensations to penetrate her completely, to float in on the warmth from the candles, to seep into her pores.

Nick pulled Sam's hands apart, guiding one hand to rest on her bare belly, the other to her shoulder.

"I bet that oil's feeling pretty slick right now. Is it hot?"

"Just warm."

"Want to heat it up?"

He slid her hand across her collarbone, stopping when her pinky touched the crisscrossed center of two thin cups of purple satin. Her fingers rested on the crest of her breast, centimeters from where her nipples peaked, straining for his touch. Her touch. Any touch.

"Your nipples are getting hard. Don't look," he said when her lashes fluttered. She complied, pressing her lids tighter. The sensations created by his voice, the warmth from the candles, the scents of the oil, overrode her need to see anything. She preferred to imagine.

"Do you ever touch yourself?"

She swallowed. "Of course."

"Have you ever touched yourself while a man watched?"

She attempted to swallow again, but there was no moisture left in her mouth. She managed to shake her head.

"Touch yourself, Samantha," he commanded, releasing her hands to quickly unhook the back of her bra. The material fell away. "Don't look, just touch." He braced his palms on her hips—flat, motionless, but raging with controlled fire that seeped straight from his skin to hers.

"You touch me, Nick."

He kissed a soft path from her shoulder to her neck, nuzzling her hair aside to nip at the lobe of her ear. "I will. Show me how."

For an instant, Sam felt dizzy. Swirls of orange and gold light danced on the dark inside of her eyelids. Nick's tongue, wet and warm, caressed the tiny spot where her pulse raged on her neck, in sync and in rhythm with the throbbing between her thighs.

She wanted to do this. Touch herself. Not for her own pleasure, that would come when he took over the task, but for his. She had the means to drive him wild with wanting; the power to stoke his pleasure beyond his most decadent imagination.

She concentrated on the feel of her oiled palms against her belly. Slowly, she smoothed a slick path across her middle then upward, coating the under-swell of her breasts with a light sheen of oil, cupping and lifting and massaging until the warm glaze covered every inch of her skin except her aureoles and nipples.

Nick's breath, ragged and hot on her neck, stopped when she said, "More oil."

Without releasing herself, she spread out her hands to accept the drops he placed on her fingertips. Licking her lips, she dabbed the hard pebbles at the center of her breasts. Sensation zinged through her, intensified Nick's hardening grip on her hips. She swirled the oil in erotic circles, outward, then back inward until she couldn't contain a pleasured coo.

Nick spun her around, lifting her with ease onto the vanity. Her eyes flashed open in time to see Nick bend his head and blow a thin stream of air directly at her nipple. The oil instantaneously reacted. The burning sensation, concentrated and focused, stole her breath. She grabbed his shoulders as he turned and ignited her other nipple.

Like the lighting of a match, the flare spread. The fire of the chemical interaction assailed her, but when Nick took her nipple in his mouth, he doused the heat on the surface of her skin only to ignite the burning deep within.

He tasted every curve and crevice of her breasts. He teased and tormented until she combed her fingers, still oily and hot, through his hair and guided his mouth to hers. Their kiss was demanding, wet. Intimate beyond belief.

The flame from a candle nipped at Sam's back, so she slid the votives to the far corners of the vanity. When she turned around, Nick had retrieved the massage oil and was shaking a generous amount into his palm. He eyed her with devilish promise.

She licked her lips. "That's an awful lot of heat you're putting into your hands."

"I have a lot of skin to cover."

"Are you going to oil yourself up for me now?" she asked hopefully.

But when his gaze dipped to her legs, then to her panties, and back to her face, that optimism died a delicious death. He meant to make sure he had touched her completely before he allowed himself the same decadent pleasure.

NICK WATCHED the anticipation light Samantha's eyes. She leaned back against the mirror, naked except for the sheer panties he planned to ask her to take off any minute. She was fearless. Brazen. At ease with her sexuality like no woman he'd ever met. And yet, he spied a hint of shyness in the way she toyed with her bottom lip with her teeth.

The experience of experimenting, of destroying the boundary between fantasy and reality, was apparently as new to her as it was to him. And he couldn't imagine a more perfect partner to share the sensations with.

He clasped his hands together to warm the chill off the bottled oil. He glanced at her panties and without saying a word, she removed them, then rebelliously crossed her legs.

He frowned.

She smiled. "I can't just give you everything you want, can I?"

"You want me to work for it?"

Through the material of his pajamas, she tickled his inner thigh with her toe. "Well, you are a known workaholic. A little effort won't kill you."

He captured her ankle before her foot reached her easy-to-find target between his legs. "I wouldn't be so sure."

Gently, he pressed her foot flat against his stomach, scooting back a few inches so she could straighten her knee. Her calves were toned and sleekly muscled, but the satiny softness of her skin provided a perfect contrast. Nick attended her foot first, massaging her from toe to heel, then her ankle, calf and knee.

By the time he reached her thigh, his control weakened and he had to fight not to pick up the pace and rush to explore the amber curls and slightly swollen flesh torturing him in the candlelit darkness.

Leaning completely against the mirror, her eyes half-closed, her thighs half-spread, she freely moaned and cooed and sighed. She threatened to drive him crazy with wanting. Resisting her was like denying his need to breathe. He splashed more oil on his hands before he caressed the soft inner flesh of her leg, moving closer to the heat he so desperately craved.

Smoothing the oil up to her outer thighs, he slowly moved forward until he stood flush with the vanity, the center of her need only inches away. Her eyes flashed wide open when his thumbs grazed the tawny triangle, thumbnails skimming the sensitive folds of flesh hidden there.

She gripped the edge of the vanity. He leaned forward, kissing her softly, enjoying the taste and tease of her mouth in nips and brushes.

"Relax, Sam."

He swished another kiss across her lips, touching her intimately with his fingers at the same time.

"You'll make me come," she admitted.

He couldn't contain a chuckle. "Yes, ma'am, I will. That's the idea."

She shook her head, grabbing his hand when he moved to touch her again. "No, I mean, if you even *touch* me again, I'll come. Right now."

"You think it's too soon?"

She nodded, biting her bottom lip with such uncertainty that Nick felt his hardened heart crack. Samantha Deveaux, his woman of experience, his woman of power, who not only knew the world, but also could conquer it with a single quip, had no idea what good loving was all about.

"Come for me, Sam. Now. Then again. And again."

With each word, he stroked her. With each successive touch, he sought her mouth. Deepening his touch. One finger. Then two. Deepening his kiss. As she predicted, the quivers started instantaneously, followed by shallow pants of breath and a tightening of her thighs around his hand until she cried out his name.

The most glorious thing he'd ever heard.

He wanted to hear it again. And again.

Slowly, he coaxed her thighs wider, massaging away the tightness in her muscles, the clenched aftermath of her release. He oiled his hands and attended her other leg while she struggled to regain her composure, rediscover her control. He had no intention of allowing that, not when wild freedom was so much more delicious.

He knelt and blew a soft breath behind her knee.

"Nick," she gasped, grabbing his shoulders as he directed the stream up along the inside of her thigh, igniting a firestorm he meant to slake with the moisture pooling in his mouth.

Her fingernails dug into his skin, a bite of pleasured pain that intensified the throb in his groin. He'd never wanted a woman so intensely, so desperately, so much that he was not only willing to wait to have her, waiting was part of the thrill. He wanted to savor her pleasure first. Make her orgasm a potent prelude to his own.

He trailed a path slowly, laving and blowing a haphazard stream of air and fire until he reached her upper thigh. Tugging gently on her ankles, he scooted her forward until her subtle scent, enriched by the aromatic oil, made him dizzy with need. He ached to taste her, but first he'd stoke the flame of her desire with a concentrated current of breath, directed at the oil-slickened cleft he so wished to savor.

"Oh. Nick. So. Hot." She punctuated each word with a writhing whimper. He braced her thighs, held her still and blew again, this time floating her name on his focused exhale.

A needful cry from her lips cut short his protracted tease. He covered her full with his mouth, cooling her at the same time that he suckled the essence of her heat. Her sweetness intoxicated him. Her pleasured cries urged him to drink until she shook again with pure, feminine release.

He stood and kissed a soothing trail from her breasts to her chin. When he met her gaze, the clouds of passion had cleared from her eyes and a seed of embarrassment threatened to shatter their intimacy. Samantha's distaste for vulnerability threatened to sever the connection they'd only begun to build, so before she bolted, he lifted her off the vanity and carried her into the shower, cradling and caressing her while he tore off his pajama pants and turned on the water.

"Nick, I..."

"Shh..." He touched a slick finger over her mouth. "No regrets, Samantha. What we're sharing is honest. Real. And there's so much more."

She closed her eyes, sighed and curled into him. Her sweet surrender touched him in a deep, uncharted recess of his heart and he hardly had the time now to figure out why. But he knew that abdication and trust didn't come easily to a woman like Sam, a woman who made her living and her reputation by staying in control. He felt honored. And the sensation nearly stole his balance along with his sanity.

When the water warmed to a pleasant heat, he carried her inside and slid the glass door shut. He dashed them both under the water, startling her into laughter, then kissing her squealing giggle into soft moans.

She broke the kiss, dipping her head back and letting the hot stream thoroughly saturate her hair. Her lashes darkened and dripped mascara down her cheeks, but he found the raccoon look adorable. However, he'd been around women long enough to know to keep that particular comment to himself.

Instead, he handed her a washcloth and soap.

"You can put me down, Nick," she said as she lathered the cloth and spread the foaming bubbles over her face.

"Then I won't be touching you."

"No, but you can watch me bathe."

He didn't need a more erotic incentive. He placed her feet on the slick tile carefully, making sure of her footing before he stepped away.

She rinsed her face clean of soap and makeup, then turned to challenge his expectant stare.

"You're too close."

"There isn't a lot of room for me to work with here, Samantha."

She glanced around him to the ledge in the corner.

"You can sit there. I've got a lot of oil to wash off. I need my space."

She sounded so practical and pragmatic, but Nick

knew by the glint in her eye and her saucy smile that she intended to do a hell of a lot more than just remove the oil he'd so carefully placed on virtually every inch of her skin. She was going to torture him.

He sat on the ledge, crossed his arms over his chest...and grinned.

She held the washcloth beneath the showerhead and rinsed away the makeup stains, then lathered again, pushing the showerhead toward the wall so the water produced steam, but left her relatively dry except for the moisture already clinging to her flesh. She stopped before touching the frothy white square to her skin and sought his hungry gaze.

"Hmm. Where should I start?"

Despite the increasing steam, Nick felt his mouth run as dry as a desert lake.

She shifted her weight from one hip to the other, seemingly engaged in perusing her body to see which part needed washing first. Glancing up, she met his gaze beneath clean but thick lashes of dark gold.

"I'm pretty much greased everywhere, aren't I?"

He attempted to swallow, gaining enough moisture to speak. "Your neck."

She slid her hand down her throat, tilting her head and arching her back so her breasts thrust deliciously forward. She raised the cloth and started slow, deliberate ministrations.

From there, she moved to her shoulders, then her arms and hands. She stepped completely out of the shower's redirected stream, so the soap clung to her like a foamy cream. From there, she washed her rib cage and belly, leaving her breasts untouched, her skin dark beside the bubbles, her nipples even darker, harder despite the warmth of the enclosed stall.

She moved to wash her ankle, but made a show of not having enough room. Grinning, she placed one foot directly between his legs on the small tiled ledge, her toes brushing his soft sac.

She massaged her foot with the cloth, brushing against his erection with seeming innocence.

"You really got that stuff all over me, didn't you?" she asked, drawing the cloth up her calf.

"I tried my best," he quipped.

She grinned. "Well, no one can ever say your best isn't good enough."

She washed her knees and thighs, drawing sensual circles on her skin. He watched each rotation, measuring the closing distance to her downy curls, spying the jutting slopes of her breasts while she moved, rhythmically, in a soft rocking motion not unlike languorous lovemaking.

But before she reached her center, she switched legs and began again.

In no hurry, she teased him more boldly this time, sliding her foot beneath him, stroking him as she washed her toes, then cruelly abandoning him to finish her leg. He used the time wisely, slipping on the condom he planned to use very, very soon.

When she stood, two places on her body remained untouched. Two places he desperately wanted to touch again. She'd taken her time bathing, and he imagined years had passed since he'd last run his hands over her breasts or felt the dewy warmth between her thighs.

Licking her lips, she boldly handed him the cloth. He

grinned, expectant and pleased. Until she turned and offered him her back.

She drew her hair over her shoulder. "I've left a couple of places for you. That's okay, right?"

He growled as he stood, snatching the cloth a little more roughly than this deliberate seduction dictated. He took a deep breath, forcing himself to wash her slowly.

"You're very, very good at this." She writhed beneath his touch, giving him precisely the incentive he needed. Samantha Deveaux was an amazing woman. Beautiful. Sensual. And smart. She played to his ego and he fell for her compliment hook, line and sinker.

Once her back was completely lathered, he stepped fully against her, his erection snug against the small of her back, his sacs gently slapping her bottom as he rocked into her. "You're not so bad yourself. You're driving me insane, Samantha."

He wrapped his arms completely around her. She sighed, lifted her arms over her shoulders and slipped her soapy hands into his hair, pulling herself ever-so-minutely upward, so that his erection slid against the soapy curve of her lower back. "I think I like you insane."

Curling his arms, he thoroughly lathered her breasts. The bubbles, a diaphanous lubricant, mingled with the oil already spread on her skin. The slick sheen on her flesh and her mindless, pleasured cries urged him to wash harder, rougher over her nipples. When she whispered his name, he dipped the cloth between her legs.

She answered his action with an unbridled, "Yes!"

He held his breath, closed his eyes and let the cloth drop to the shower floor so he could spread the soap with his fingers. Her feminine folds were slick and hot. The wet warmth that curled around his hand came not from the water or the foam, but from the intimate place deep within her, the place he longed to greet with his own insatiable need.

She bent forward just enough to invite his erection between her legs. She stroked and manipulated his pulsing head into her slippery passage.

Nick groaned as he slid inside. She felt like hot velvet on a cold night, completely enveloping him in a sensation that was comfortable and warm, then instantly turned scalding to the point of pain. The instinct to drive hard—to reach her core and release the delights hidden there—was nearly impossible to fight, but he struggled and won. Gently, he guided her hands onto the marble wall, where the misdirected showerhead spewed a steamy spray that forced them both to close their eyes or be blinded by the shardlike mist.

Then Samantha started to move, rocking with an undeniable rhythm—an irresistible tempo that pulsed straight to the part of him that was nothing but pure and simple male need. He matched her movements, echoed her pleasured cries until even the powerful water swirling around them was no match for the tempest they created.

With unbridled thrusts, Nick gave Samantha every inch of him. With indulgent moans, she took what he gave, then slipped one hand off the wall and wrapped her fingers around the back of his neck, pulling herself closer. Forcing him deeper. Destroying every flailing thought in his mind except one.

Join.

Their climax was loud and long and followed by sensuous strokes and soft words and eventually, a gentle, mutual laughter. Nick pulled the showerhead from the wall and rinsed Sam clean of soap. She did the same to him, then flipped the faucet off. A thick fog surrounded them. Ensconced in the mystic, dreamlike cloud, Nick silently wondered if any of this was real. Samantha. The free, limitless boundaries of their lovemaking.

The emotions raging through him. Admiration. Wonder. Excitement.

Sam slipped her arms around his waist and laid her head on his chest. "That was new."

"You've never showered with a lover before?"

Sam leaned back and glanced up at him with a wounded look so exaggerated, he knew she was simply reverting to her natural inclination to tease him. "How many lovers do you think I've had?"

He kissed her impertinent nose. "Don't know. Don't care."

One golden eyebrow tilted and he could see she wasn't entirely convinced. "What about you? You've never showered with any of your lovers before?"

Nick laughed aloud at the idea of Blair allowing her makeup to run or her hair to get wet—or Sophia agreeing to lovemaking anywhere except the confines of a bed. He'd had other lovers, of course, but none of those women had ever enticed him to share anything so personal, so erotic.

"I can honestly say this was a fantastic first."

The pride that lit Samantha's eyes rewarded him for his honesty. Her next suggestion was a good old-fashioned, New Orleans styled lagniappe. Something extra. Something unexpected.

"Care to try for a second?"

10

AROUND 4:00 A.M., they stopped counting. Sam listened to Nick sleeping, her head tucked in the crook of his arm, his hard pectoral muscle softened by a downy pillow. She closed her eyes, determined to sleep, determined to keep her mind from analyzing all that had happened between them—all the intimacies they'd discovered and shared, both physical and spiritual. In between their lovemaking, they'd polished off the strawberries and the bottle of sparkling wine while he told her about his family. About his responsibilities to his family. About his utter devotion to making sure his company was so solvent, so successful, that if anyone in the LaRocca line ever needed anything money could buy, he'd have no trouble providing the cash.

Sam shifted in Nick's sleeping arms, marveling at all she'd learned in one rather brief conversation. From his confident demeanor, she'd assumed the LaRoccas had always had money—always enjoyed success. She'd been surprised to discover that Nick came from humble roots—that his grandmothers hadn't started their business in earnest until ten years ago, when the restaurant they ran in Chicago's theatre district stumbled onto hard times. Fresh out of business school, Nick had helped his Nanas build an empire that not only put the restaurant back on its feet, but also provided incomes for every family member who wanted a job.

He was barely thirty-five, but he had become the patriarch of a tightly woven fabric of family. No wonder he was willing to work so hard to keep it all together.

A smudge of praline sauce, cool after they'd extinguished the Sterno, had dropped onto her lap, effectively stopping any further conversation. Then a while later, sated by food, drink and sex, they found themselves in his bed and Nick asked Samantha to reciprocate with stories of her own. But she'd effectively distracted him with coos and kisses until tales of her home life were no longer important to him.

Then, he'd fallen asleep, leaving Samantha to wonder how much, if anything, she should tell him when he woke.

Unable to put the matter to rest, Sam slid out of bed and into one of the terry-cloth robes they'd left on the floor. She inhaled the lapel, trying to determine who'd worn the garment last, but their scents were so intermingled, she couldn't tell. The entwined fragrances of his shampoo, her perfume, the massage oil and sweet, browned sugar engendered an immediate melancholy Sam didn't want to feel.

Tonight was about tonight, she reminded herself. No commitments. No regrets. Pleasure for the moment. In the moment.

Despite the robe, she shivered.

She slipped into the outer room, dark except for the lights on Poydras Street glowing through the wall of windows on the other side of the conference table. She poured herself a snifter of cognac and slid her hip onto the credenza beside the window, staring out onto the business district, a portion of the city she barely knew. Yet even if her view was of the French Quarter, she wouldn't have known much more. She'd been away for so long. Too long. She'd come home to find her roots, connections to her family and her past that had been ripped and torn during her parents' divorce.

What she'd found instead was a man she could love, if only he didn't have to leave. If only he didn't have responsibilities and interests that would inevitably and rightfully be more important than her.

She'd lived that kind of life with her father. Devlin Deveaux always had a big studio, a crew of technicians and actors, a career milestone that came before she did on his list of priorities. He depended on her to understand, to pick up the slack and pay the electric bill and fix his breakfast and make sure the housekeeper had his laundry done. She'd developed an interest in the film industry only to be closer to him. Hell, if she dug a little deeper, she'd admit that she'd only moved in with Anthony, the star of her father's latest, highest-budget film, to get a reaction out of Devlin—maybe some anger or a touch of concern that she'd risk her heart with such a well-known heartbreaker.

Instead, he'd been thrilled that she was keeping his headliner happy. Not that she hadn't truly been attracted to Anthony. His perfect features and devastating smile made him impossible for any woman to resist. She'd even grown to respect him as an actor and care for him as a good friend. But when the photos of their limousine tryst came to light, he'd considered allowing their release simply to further his career. Publicity was, after all, publicity. Good or bad.

She'd finally convinced him to change his mind, but the damage to their relationship was done. He was no better than her father, willing to sacrifice her for his own needs.

She'd sworn she'd never again involve herself with anyone—a man especially—who might even entertain the notion of using her to get what they wanted.

Yet, hadn't she invited Nick to do exactly the same thing?

Her thoughts weren't so deep or indulgent that she didn't sense him all the way across the room the minute he appeared in the doorway. After all they'd shared, she knew she'd detect his undeniable presence even in the largest crowd. He paused in the threshold a moment, fully nude and glorious, then strode across the darkness as if he wore a designer tuxedo. His self-assurance acted like a magnet to her wounded, restless heart and she could feel a renewed desire to reach out for his attention.

She shook her head and took a sip of the brandy, suspecting she'd need the full breadth of her resistance to fight the elemental, emotional pull Nick cast over her. Heat burned down her throat, settling the quivers that shook her as he approached.

"Aren't you exhausted?" he asked.

"Too tired to sleep, I guess." She attempted a smile, but the action only provoked a deepening of Nick's furrowed expression.

"What's wrong? No, wait. Stupid question for any

man to ask a woman. You'll just say, 'nothing,' and we're back to square one."

As much as she fought the reaction, his dead-on observation evoked a genuine smile.

"You have a busy day ahead of you, Nick. Go back to sleep. I'll just finish this and then join you."

He slipped into the space between the credenza and a potted palm, his naked thighs brushing against her knees. "You have a busy day, too. Following me around. Pretending to be my lover."

"Guess that won't tax my acting abilities anymore, will it?"

She knocked back the last of the cognac, then handed him the glass and moved to slip off her perch on the credenza. He thwarted her sudden need to escape by caressing her cheek with his palm, touching her with a gentleness that held her still.

"Is this about regrets, Samantha?"

Without thinking, she pressed her face closer to his hand. *Without thinking.* Her instincts, primal and strong, lured her to this man like a lioness to her chosen mate. He could sate her hunger. He could ensure the continued survival of her womanhood, the element of her body, soul and spirit that dictated the feminine needs she'd ignored for so long.

"I don't regret making love with you, Nick. But that doesn't mean I'm certain it was a wise choice. For either of us."

Nick slid the empty snifter onto the windowsill then brushed a lock of her hair out of her face and twirled it around her ear. The sensation of his fingertip, rough against the sensitive skin, evoked a renewed flame deep within her. A flickering pulse sparked between her legs. Her nipples tightened and she couldn't help but sigh.

God help her. She was farther gone than she realized.

Nick drew a lazy line from her earlobe, beneath her chin, then up until he traced the soft curves of her mouth. "Did we really have a choice?"

She shook her head, determined to defy the sensual spell he wove. "We always have a choice."

"Do we? Really?" With each word, he lowered his face. Inch by inch, his mouth neared hers. She searched his gaze for any hint of machination, any spark of untruth in what he said or did that would give her the means to elude him, to protect her heart before she fell too far into the well of need.

But just as his lashes closed over his dark green gaze, she saw nothing but pure, raw desire. With his kiss, she succumbed to the craving—concentrated and intense. She was too tired to fight, too overwhelmed to struggle.

In the morning, she'd use the dawn to show him that they had no business opening this Pandora's box of unfettered desire. Nothing lasting could come of their pairing. After the ecstasy wore away, they'd have nothing but emptiness.

In the morning. Because right now, with Nick's hands slowly pushing her robe aside and his mouth trailing a hot path to her breasts, Samantha had never felt so full.

"ROOM SERVICE," the voice responded. After yesterday, Nick knew better than to fall for that ruse again, but this time the voice was familiar. Very familiar. Like a voice he'd been hearing his entire life. His lungs clenched. A pit formed in his throat.

No. Not here. Not today.

He said a brief prayer before he peered through the peephole, then swore up at heaven for having no mercy.

Nana Rose.

"Dominick Michael LaRocca, you open this door this instant!" When she started muttering in Italian, Nick unhinged the lock, took a deep breath and pulled open the door with a patient smile.

"Nana Rose, what are you doing here?"

Her pointed glare erased the bogus grin off his face, though he still bent forward for the obligatory kiss on the cheek. They'd barely exchanged the greeting when his grandmother made a startling snuffling noise and waved past him. "What am I doing here? What am I doing here?" Her volume escalated with each repetition. "I'm sitting in my easy chair, bottom of the ninth, Cubs up by one and the scoring run on third base when WGN scrolls a little news flash across the bottom of my screen. Good thing Fae insisted we buy the big-screen television for the ball games. I'd have missed it, so small."

"Missed?"

Her harrumph and iced stare told him she knew about his involvement with Samantha. He started forward to explain, but she put a stop to that with one palm-out gesture.

"Stay at the door!" she ordered, her petite form waddling beneath a covered tray of *sciaccata*, the thick-doughed pizza she brought with her whenever she visited anyone, anywhere. "Rafaela and Anita are right behind me. They stopped in Anita's suite to drop off our bags."

She popped the tray right on top of the papers he'd been looking over while Samantha showered and dressed in his room. He listened, but from this distance he couldn't hear the water running or determine if she knew they were no longer alone. He'd shut the door for precisely that purpose. He was finding it hard enough getting any work done with so little sleep and an hour-long interview with the police. Just the sound of her turning on the water had his body instantly ready to relive the sensuous washing they'd shared the night before. But he'd already scheduled a meeting with Anita to review the vital numbers for the European distribution deal. When he'd called her room to cancel, even at the ungodly hour of 6:00 a.m., she hadn't answered her phone.

Now he knew why. She'd been summoned to fetch their grandmothers and hadn't done a damn thing to warn him.

"Anita knew you were coming?"

Rose smiled, flipping off the striped cloth that hid his favorite food underneath. The scents of garlic, Romano cheese and olive oil wafted into the air. Real Italian pizza from the Old World.

"Of course not. We called her midflight to pick us up."

Nick swore under his breath, but his grandmother scolded him with piercing eyes nonetheless.

He thrust his hands on his hips and scowled back. Disrespectful or not, every once in a while he had to remind his meddlesome grandmother that he was no longer a little boy. "So you heard about Samantha and couldn't get here fast enough to check her out."

Rose shook her finger at him. "Watch your tone, Dominick. We're here because we have business to discuss."

Nick's spine reverberated with the serious tone of her voice. Nana Rose rarely, if ever, got truly angry. Fits of temper were usually left for Rafaela, the younger of the two by a year or so. Though the women only became related when Nick's father married Nick's mother, they'd been inseparable friends since their childhood in Sicily. Their families had come over to America together just before the First World War. Rose and Fae had attended the same schools, learned English together, discovered cooking in the same kitchens, had even, by their own embellished accounts, been courted by some of the same men.

After Rose married Vincente LaRocca and Fae wed Salvatore Durante, they continued their friendship until they successfully arranged for their two eldest children to fall in love. Nick's parents, who'd remained silent about the grandmothers' scheme to find Nick a wife, often joked about being the last arranged marriage in the New World. But the truth was, they'd been married for over forty years and were still going strong.

Now Rose and Fae had their sights set on Nick, and no doubt, they weren't happy that he'd gone and found a woman without consulting them first.

"There he is!"

Rounding the corner in the hallway with Anita cradling her thin arm, Nana Fae was all smiles and kisses when she crossed the threshold.

"Oh! This is a lovely room. Look at the view, Rose."

"I'd rather look at what Signore Lover-boy has planned for the European distribution of our marinara line," Nana Rose replied, with a tad more snip than his grandmother normally employed.

Nick shut the door, perplexed. He shot Anita a look that begged for some help, but she shrugged her shoulders and shook her head, obviously as confused as he was.

The introduction of LaRocca products into the overseas market had been Nick's idea from the beginning, and until today, his worry. His grandmothers normally concerned themselves more with recipes and promotion, leaving placement and distribution issues entirely up to Nick and Anita. The notion of taking an Italian-American product into the European marketplace—where genuine foods from Italy were commonplace—was a calculated risk, but one Nick was convinced would take LaRocca to the next level of worldwide success.

Unfortunately, to breach the tight market, Nick had to do business with the most powerful food distributor in Italy, one Franco Bomini. Though raised in the United States, Franco had returned to his birthplace in Rome to launch a billion-dollar brokerage business. Bomini, who grew up in the same Taylor Street neighborhood as his grandparents, was violently disliked by both the LaRocca and the Durante clans. Nick never pressed for details, figuring that the past was the past, and so long as his grandmothers didn't expressly object, he could solicit the man's business without worrying about whatever personal rancor existed between the man and Nick's family.

But now, with Nana Fae oddly quiet at one end of the conference table and Nana Rose practically ranting at the other, he was worried. Very, very worried.

"You made me promise to handle the Bomini deal myself," Nick reminded Rose. "You didn't want to be involved. Why the interest all of a sudden?"

Rose's dark eyes narrowed into slits. "Because I'm not the only one who watches the Cubs play baseball."

Nick took over for Anita, helping Fae, who had trouble with her knees, sit in a comfortable chair, with arms, at the conference table.

"*Grazie*, Dominick," Fae spoke, patting his cheek lovingly. "Rosalia, *sederie*."

As Fae ordered, Rose accepted Dominick's proffered chair.

Anita busied herself making a fresh pot of coffee at the wet bar. Nick, sideswiped by his grandmothers' sudden arrival, chose to stand near the window and lean against the same credenza Samantha had retreated to when he found her missing from his bed last night. Her look had been sad and pensive, but she'd responded to his touch with an eagerness that belied his first suspicion that she regretted their lovemaking.

But if she didn't regret their liaison last night, she surely would once she came through that still-closed bedroom door. He tried to devise a means to warn her...then realized that her presence in his suite, with his grandmothers, the matchmakers, there as witnesses, was *exactly* what he should want.

Suddenly, he was torn. Protect Samantha or thwart his grandmothers' marriage scheme? He didn't realize how conflicting those goals would be. To save him from the unwanted attention of strangers, he'd have to sacrifice Samantha's reputation. He didn't like the cost one damn bit.

But Rose interrupted his thoughts by rapping on the table. "I got a call last night just as that no-good second baseman struck out and left the runner stranded at third."

Nick nodded. The Cubs had lost again, which accounted for part of his grandmother's foul mood.

"And this is related to our distribution how?"

"Franco Bomini..." Rose paused after speaking the name, as if she might spit to remove the bad taste from her mouth "...was in Chicago last night, visiting his new great-granddaughter."

Nick's gut clenched. "Bomini is in the States?"

Rose nodded, her mouth in a grim line. "He stayed up late to watch the game with his son-in-law, when all of a sudden he reads that you are romantically involved with some woman you picked up at the Food Expo."

Nick checked his temper even as his blood raged. He didn't like the tone of his grandmother's voice, the implication that Samantha was nothing but some stranger he'd met in a crowd.

She had been only that when they'd first met— God, less than twenty-four hours ago. But even before they'd made love, she'd already become more to him.

How? He had no idea. And he certainly couldn't work the logic through with his grandmothers staring up at him with disapproving eyes.

"First of all, Samantha Deveaux is a lovely woman," he clarified. "She saved my life, no thanks to you two. Your little practical joke has women tearing at my clothes and literally jumping out from under my bed. I won't even tell you about the naked nuns in the lobby."

Fae giggled while Rose crossed herself to ward off any possible blasphemy. Nick looked up in time to see Anita slip seamlessly into his bedroom.

"Well, maybe Fae and I acted a bit rashly, but the truth is, Dominick, you *have* to settle down. Now more than ever. You know how Franco feels about indiscriminate personal behavior."

Nick dug his hands into his pockets. "Yes, he's very European. Marriage is a must. Mistresses are also a must, but should be kept discreetly."

Even Rose sniggered at his true assessment of Bomini's continental attitude. Fae remained quiet. While his grandmother Rose and her husband, Vincente, made no secret of their personal dislike for the man, they knew enough about the food business to know that only Bomini could break their American company into the European market. Fae remained, as always, totally silent on the matter. So far as Nick knew, she wouldn't even speak Bomini's name.

"According to the video on the evening news, you and this Miss Deveaux have not been very discreet. Bomini can't see how he should do business with a man who flaunts his romances on the television."

Nick took a deep breath. Now was not the time to point out, yet again, that he wouldn't be in this situation if his grandmothers hadn't schemed to force his marriage.

"I suppose you want me to fly to Chicago and smooth his ruffled feathers."

"No need," Rose said, waving her hand. "He's coming here."

"To New Orleans?"

Nick asked the question at the same time as Nana Fae. Her eyes were filled with something akin to terror, an emotion he'd never seen in his indomitable grandmother's gaze.

"Why do you think we flew down in the middle of the night? To bring you *scacciata* and meet your new lady friend?"

Nick stared, eyes wide, needing nothing verbal to acknowledge the obvious.

"Well, of course we did that, too. So, where is she?"

As if on cue, the door to the bedroom opened and Samantha emerged, a slight stumble in her first step as if she'd been pushed. Anita poked her head out from behind her, folding her lips together to contain a raging fit of laughter.

Nick shook his head, then massaged his forehead. When he looked up, both his grandmothers were staring at him, perplexed and impatient.

He did the honors with less enthusiasm than he should have. "Nana Rose, Nana Fae, this is Samantha Deveaux."

Sam smiled. "It's a pleasure to meet you both."

Anita scurried to the wet bar to pour cups of coffee

and serve them to their grandmothers, still quiet as they assessed Samantha from head to toe. Dressed for their scheduled lunch appointment with the head of a Northwest grocery chain, she wore a black turtleneck and blazer, blue jeans and boots. With her hair pulled back in a ponytail and her face sporting just enough makeup to bring out her luminous eyes and generous lips, she looked as vivacious and athletic as she'd proved to be in his bed, and as casual and comfortable in her own skin as any woman he'd ever known.

He smiled, confident that his grandmothers would like her, then frowned, wondering why in the hell that should suddenly be important to him.

Rose turned and whispered over her shoulder. "She stayed here last night?"

Nick cast an unrepentant grin at his Nana. "This is the twenty-first century, Nana."

"Yes, well, women stayed the night with men in my century, too," Rose countered. "Difference was, in the morning, you married them, or their brothers hunted you down with a gun."

"Do you have brothers, dear?" Fae asked, not as innocently as she intended. Anita didn't bother to hide a snicker and Rose huffed her disapproval at being thwarted.

Sam had the dignity to hide her smile. "No, ma'am. I have a sister, though. She lives here in New Orleans, but she's on her honeymoon."

"How sweet. *Per favore*, come sit beside me."

Samantha joined Fae without hesitation, giving Rose an extra-wide smile before she sat. "This is a little awkward," she admitted, instantaneously earning Fae's sympathy judging by the look on his grandmother's face.

Nick was impressed. One down, one to go.

"Of course it is. We don't usually barge in on Dominick," Fae said, turning her head toward Rose, her expression brimming with chastisement. "And we won't again. But now that we're here, tell us a little about yourself."

"The news said your mother is a psychic?" Rose asked, her tone slightly skeptical.

Sam grinned. "Yes, ma'am. I'm afraid I don't come from a conventional family. My father is Devlin Deveaux, the film director."

As the conversation grew and expanded, Nick circled over to the bar, watching as Sam slowly but surely won his grandmothers' approval. She was honest, funny, forthcoming and respectful. She asked questions about Rose and Fae's other grandchildren, about their lives in Chicago and their childhoods in Sicily. She even admitted a little more than he expected about her life in Hollywood—and the lack of family ties that bothered her most.

After an hour had passed, they'd shared Rose's pizza, coffee and a good dose of mutual liking. When Sam excused herself to freshen up before they left for their appointment, Nick exhaled a confident breath. If nothing else, his worries about his grandmothers' meddling in his private life, at least for the moment, were over. If they liked Samantha as much as he suspected, they'd soon call off their quest to find him a wife.

"So," he said confidently, "I take it you find her as charming as I do."

"Very much so, Dominick," Fae said, smiling. "It's no wonder you forgot your upbringing and took her to bed the first night you met her."

Anita spat out her coffee. Nick had a damn hard time swallowing the last of his. While Rose was infamous for her straight-to-the-heart-of-the-matter assessments, Fae was usually more discreet.

She silenced them both with a nonchalant wave. *"Va' la, non fare l'innocentino."*

Nick and Anita obeyed, wiping the "so innocent butter would melt in their mouths" look off their faces.

"Things don't work so differently in this twenty-first century of yours as it did in ours," Rose said. "You've bedded her. Ordinarily, that's a private matter between the two of you."

"Ordinarily?"

With a nod, Rose opened her basket-weave purse and produced a folded document. The blue back page told Nick it was something legal. When he took the pages from his grandmother, he recognized the contract he'd signed when his grandmothers appointed him chief executive officer of the company.

"Read section eight, sub-paragraph C," Rose instructed.

Nick tore at the pages until he found the section she indicated. He'd read each and every word of the contract before he signed it six years ago. Hadn't he? The words blurred, first with disbelief and then with anger.

Words like *moral turpitude*, *scandalous* and *family values* jumped out at him.

"A morals clause?" he bit out. He didn't remember signing this. He knew he had, but he'd probably ignored the clause in deference to his Old World grandmothers and their Old World ideas.

Both Rose and Fae met his outrage with stoic faces. "An insurance policy." Rose stood, her gnarled fingers braced on the table. "Fae and I worked too long and too hard to lose this company to scandal. You made a spectacle of your affair with Miss Deveaux. Now, you'll make it right."

She gestured for Fae to gather her things and then waddled behind her to help her stand.

"What do you mean 'make it right'?"

After Rose was certain Fae had her balance, she looked up and skewered him with a pointed stare. "Has the English language changed so much with the new century? You'll make it right. You'll marry her and keep this scandal from embarrassing the family. You'll marry her or you'll lose your job."

11

GET MARRIED? Sam clamped her hand over her mouth. She didn't know whether to feel guilty for eavesdropping or indulge in the hysterics she held tight in her belly. She contained her laughter, not wanting the family to hear her outburst. She was certain that, to them, this situation wasn't the least bit humorous.

She pressed her ear to the bedroom door, trying to decipher the raised voices, then realized most of the conversation had now lapsed into the LaRoccas' native tongue. Since her knowledge of Italian ended at *ciao, baby*, Samantha numbly paced to the bed and sat.

Nick had to marry her or lose his job?

Her wonder at the irony lasted for about ten seconds. With all the talk that had gone around that conference table about this being the twenty-first century, the archaic clause shouldn't be causing any friction at all. The obvious solution to this problem resided with her, and she'd take care of this mess right now, before Nick said something to his grandmothers that he might regret—or vice versa. She marched into the fray with a patient smile and stood there, rocking on her heels with her hands clasped behind her back until Rose, Fae, Anita and Nick all acknowledged her presence with testy stares.

She rewarded them with the sweetest smile she

could muster. "Sorry to interrupt." She made sure her voice reflected only a tiny ounce of true apology. Nick and Anita might be accustomed to being pushed around by their grandmothers, but adorable and well meaning though they were, Sam couldn't allow her future to be dictated by strangers. She had enough trouble with her own mother, who'd attempted to speed Sam's involvement in a committed relationship along with an engagement ring, massage oil and some condoms. Maybe Endora was truly clairvoyant. They'd already indulged in the oil and prophylactics. Now she had a way to use her great-grandmother's jewelry as well.

"Samantha, you don't have to get involved," Nick assured her. He swiped his hand through his hair and took a deep, apparently fortifying breath. "I'll handle this."

She didn't doubt Nick could make this situation go away, but she didn't know what the outcome would do to his relationship with his family. Her method was quicker. Cleaner.

"There's nothing to handle, Nick."

She slipped her great-grandmother's ruby ring off her right hand where she'd put it this morning for safekeeping. With a purposeful march, she handed Nick the ring. "Ask me to marry you."

"What?"

She pursed her lips. When his rage kept him from recognizing her subtle hint, she winked. "You heard your grandmothers. You don't want to lose your job, do you? Ask me to marry you."

Nick blinked several times. He hesitated, but began to do as she asked, perhaps out of curiosity alone.

"Will you—"

"Oh, no," she stopped him, simply because she could. A trill of excitement, of expectant pleasure, surged through her. This might be all make-believe, but Sam was an expert in that department. Besides, this might be the only proposal she ever got. "Down on one knee. I do have my standards."

Behind him, Nick's grandmothers quietly nodded. Oh, how she hated to disappoint them.

Nick complied, taking her left hand in his. "Samantha Deveaux, will you do me the honor of becoming my wife?"

For the briefest instant, Sam allowed her imagination to shift her into a romantic dream where she had brought Nick to his knees in want of her. Where he lifted her into his arms after her teary-eyed acceptance and carried her to the bed to make mad, passionate love.

Only in the movies, she mused. Except for the mad, passionate love part, which she figured would soon be over for good.

"No," she answered.

"What?" Rose nearly broke a hip thrusting her fists in outrage. Fae, like Anita, merely covered her mouth to contain a laugh.

"I won't marry him. He asked. I declined. He's done his duty by your morals clause. That contract can't force me to become his wife, can it? And really, Mrs. LaRocca, that's a dirty trick to play on your grandson. Especially one who loves you both so much."

With a gentle tug, Sam helped Nick stand. He gazed down at her and his expression stole her breath. Was he disappointed? Amused? Hurt? Damn, she couldn't tell. He brushed a soft kiss across her cheek, then turned to his grandmothers and gestured with a flourish.

"There you go," he concluded.

Rose threw up her hands, thwarted again but not down for the count. She gazed at Samantha intensely, but Sam knew her act of defiance had raised her in Rose's esteem. She could see the respect in the older woman's focused gaze.

"That doesn't solve our problem with Franco Bomini," Rose said. "He may have the morals of an alley cat, but he doesn't do business with people he doesn't respect. Right now, he's looking for an excuse *not* to do business with us."

"Putting Dominick's picture on our pasta sauce played right into his hands." Fae waved to Anita to help her sit again, this time choosing the more comfortable love seat, indicating to Sam that a LaRocca family strategy session was about to ensue.

"I should check on security for your meeting, Nick." Sam noted the time on her watch. Since she'd just declined an offer to officially join the LaRocca family, she thought it best to make herself scarce. "We're scheduled to leave in an hour."

Rose scuttled beside Fae and lowered herself into the cushions. "No, no, young lady. I think we need you here. It's clear you don't appreciate other people making decisions for you. You're a quick thinker. We may need your help."

Sam smiled at the compliment, wondering if she could ever convince her mother of her ample intelligence or her need for independence so easily. She'd come home to attempt to repair the rift her parents' divorce had caused between her and her family, and yet, sitting down with the LaRoccas, obvious experts in family values, she realized that her moves toward true reconciliation with her mother had been nothing more than lip service. To mend the damage, they'd actually have to have a conversation. Maybe even a loud fight instead of sharp barbs and innuendos.

But for now, Sam slid onto the recliner across from Nick's grandmothers, determined to help them however she could, save marrying her grandson and moving to Chicago.

"Is Mr. Bomini a superstitious man?" Sam asked.

Fae looked down at her hands while Rose twisted her mouth in thought. "Of course. No self-respecting Italian man isn't afraid of a good curse. Are you planning to call your mother?"

Sam shook her head. Endora wasn't too keen on curses. She preferred to deal with only positive forces and clean, white magic. *What the hell was she thinking?* Sam didn't believe in her mother's mumbo jumbo. But asking for her mother's help—willingly—might be a gesture to benefit them all.

"I will call her if we need her, but she doesn't really do curses. But she might, under special circumstances. I was just throwing out ideas. Brainstorming."

Rose nodded, smiling. "Trust me, Samantha. I don't need a psychic to deliver a potent curse. But you should call your mother anyway."

"Why?"

"She's your mother, isn't she?"

Sam nodded, unnerved that Nick's grandmothers had the same intuitive powers her mother owned without all the costumes and drama. Did women achieve some special power just by giving birth? Sam shook her head, confusion and anxiety building with each passing moment. The fact that Nick stood just behind her, silent, didn't help. His pensive vibrations echoed through her—from the tense set of his shoulders to his measured circular pace.

She glanced over her shoulder, attempting a peek at his expression. He turned just as she did, denying her a clear view of his face.

Nick toyed with the ruby ring Sam had handed him, aware that she watched him. Practice allowed him to keep his face emotionless. Stoic. He was angry. Damn angry. Though her spontaneous and brilliant charade of a refused proposal had thwarted his grandmothers and effectively saved his job, the aftermath unnerved him. He simply didn't like it when someone told him no, that was all. Right? Even in pretense, Dominick LaRocca didn't get on his knees just to be denied.

Or did his fury stem from somewhere deeper? For a brief, unreal instant, he'd secretly hoped Samantha would consent to be his wife. Until last night, he'd thought that the woman he'd been seeking for a soul mate was nothing like Samantha. That their affair was a mutually beneficial dalliance. A way to pleasurably pass the time.

In marriage, he'd wanted a woman who was quiet. No opinions of her own, except for those he couldn't be bothered with. Someone who would mold her life to fit his demanding, important schedule.

How boring. How arrogant. As Anita had pointed out yesterday, he'd found his so-called dream woman with Sophia, and while she was admittedly too extreme, he should have learned his lesson. In his mind, he'd conjured up a woman that would be impossible to find so he didn't have to bother with looking. With being disappointed. Or with becoming trapped.

Marriages, even to an amazingly independent, intelligent, caring and compassionate woman like Samantha demanded the one thing Nick had a hell of a hard time mastering—compromise. Sharing. Surrendering his needs to fulfill the desires of his partner. In lovemaking, he handled the concept with relish. Enjoyed it even. But in life? He wanted everything and he wanted it all his way.

He was spoiled. Hardworking and loyal, yes, but spoiled nonetheless. Yet he was trapped at the same time. Snared more firmly than a snake in a tiger pit by a woman who had, with her refusal, held firm to their agreement of no commitments or promises beyond the weekend.

"I have an idea," Nick said, slowly spinning the glittering red-jeweled ring on his pinkie. He closed his eyes and swallowed, only half believing what he was about to suggest. Talk about a gamble. Nick shook his head, knowing that if he thought too hard, he might change his mind. Maybe he needed to take a second lesson from Samantha. As a stuntwoman, she'd had the courage to jump off buildings and hang from window ledges one hundred feet above the ground. But this wasn't the movies. Nick was a man of reality. A believer in the bottom line.

"Are you going to share with the rest of us?" Anita asked.

He was going to share all right. On a trial basis, anyway. He was going to share until sharing killed him. That's how much he wanted Samantha in his life.

"Bomini will only be here for today, right?" he asked. "The Expo ends tomorrow."

Rose nodded. "He has to be back in Rome by Monday. That he told me."

"Then Sam and I can just pretend to be married until then."

"Pretend?" Sam asked.

Nick slid around to the front of Samantha's chair. Determined to work this spin correctly, he knelt back down in front of her, the ring clutched between his fingers.

"It's not like the man is going to demand a marriage certificate. It's not like I'd feel the least compelled to show him one even if he did. But if I tell him we flew off to Vegas last night to marry, he has no choice but to believe me. I'm a man of my word."

"You won't be after you tell him that lie," Samantha pointed out. It was apparent to him that her skepticism ran deeper than her expression revealed. They may have known each other for only a day, but already Nick could sense more about her than he could with anyone else. He read pure unadulterated fear in her gaze. Fear of him. Fear of them together.

Good. He didn't want to be the only one quaking in his boots.

Fae finally spoke up. "Franco Bomini wouldn't know the truth if it bit him on his..." She spat out the Italian word for backside with more spite than Nick had ever heard from his grandmother before. Maybe he shouldn't go through with this. No distribution deal was worth the stress his grandmother obviously felt. No matter how much the pretense of marriage could help him win Samantha's heart and the distribution deal as well, he wouldn't sacrifice his grandmother for either victory. He'd find another way.

"Then let's find someone else to distribute our products," Nick said. "Bomini isn't the only game in town. He's the most powerful, but—"

Fae stamped her foot and pointed at him with a crooked finger. "Don't coddle me, Dominick. Bomini deserves to be lied to. It'll serve him right, the hypocrite."

Nick jerked at his grandmother's poisoned tone, but suddenly felt righteous in perpetuating this untruth. For Rafaela's sake. For the sake of the LaRocca family.

For him and Samantha. If nothing else, the charade could win him one more night in her arms, one more night to brand himself in her heart.

"What do you say? I'm asking again and I'm already on my knees."

Sam drew her bottom lip in her mouth. "You just want me to *pretend* to be your wife. For the weekend?"

Nick held the ring out to her, twirling it so the facets caught the light. "Maybe your mother *is* psychic. She sent the ring, didn't she?"

"Don't even joke about that," she said, the power of her chastising deflated by the sound of genuine fear.

Again, the sound of her apprehension bolstered his determination. If Nick was going to start sharing, he thought it only fair to give Sam half of both the good and the bad.

SAMANTHA SLIPPED INTO the restaurant ladies' room just before dinner, alone, not knowing where Nick had disappeared to during appetizers and drinks, and willing herself not to care. Just before they'd left the hotel for the dinner party Anita had hastily arranged at Brennan's, Nick fired her as his bodyguard. Television and radio stations across the country had announced the end of Nick's bachelor status. Reporters interviewed women who'd been chasing him and noted that the hunt was officially over. Pictures of Samantha and Nick, posing and smiling beneath a floral wedding arch they'd borrowed from the hotel, had made their way onto the Internet. So far as the world knew, she was the new Mrs. Dominick LaRocca.

At least her moviemaking, media-spinning knowhow had come in handy. But she swallowed the irony with the same resistance as a thick dose of chalky antacid. She'd come home to New Orleans to escape Hollywood's pretense, to discover what was real and true and important. She'd found love—and it was all a lie.

"The bodyguard hides in the bathroom. That would make an interesting headline."

Samantha turned at the sound of an opening door, not in the least surprised to see her mother enter the small bathroom as if she were a queen entering her royal hall. Her timing, as always, was impeccable. Endora locked the door, then sashayed over to the mirror to check her flaming red, perfectly coiffed and curled hair.

"I'm not his bodyguard anymore. He fired me."

"He paid you first, I hope."

Sam nodded. No Chances Protection was safe from bankruptcy, Nick had seen to that. And since she'd received a call from Serena announcing her and Brandon's arrival in New Orleans by tomorrow afternoon, Sam's professional life was finally looking up. If only her personal life would follow suit.

"How did you know where to find me?" Samantha asked, knowing her mother's crystal ball didn't usually operate as a homing device.

"I received a phone call from a charming woman, Rosalia LaRocca. She invited me to attend the dinner as her guest. I haven't met her yet, but her granddaughter, Anita, told me I'd find you hiding in here."

"I'm not hiding."

"Oh? Then what are you doing, Samantha?"

"Don't you know?"

Endora pressed her red-rouged lips together in a thin line, crossing her arms across her amble bosom with a jangle of bracelets and beads. "Do you want to know what I see when I look at you?"

Sam slid off the porcelain sink where she'd perched. "No, Mother, not really. I may not share your psychic talents, but I'm pretty sure I already know what you see."

"Really? And what is that?"

Sam shook her head, pressing her lashes together tightly to fight the burning tears welling behind her eyes. Of all the places to have this conversation with her mother. The bathroom of a restaurant! On the eve of her biggest heartbreak.

"You see the daughter you love, the daughter who abandoned you, the daughter who can't seem to make anything work in her life."

Endora shook her head and sighed. "Good thing I'm the only one who depends on intuition to make a decent living." Endora opened her arms, but Sam shook her head. She couldn't hug her mother right now. If she'd did, she'd lose control and she feared she'd never get it back.

Endora took her refusal in stride. "You're right on only one thing, Samantha. I do love you. Yes, I resented the fact that you chose to live with your father after the divorce." Her face twisted in an expression half-disgusted and half-amused. "Five years old and had a mind of your own. But I never meant to make you feel guilty for that."

Sam skewered her mother with a pointed look.

"Okay, maybe I meant to make you feel a little guilty."

Sam nodded at her victory, hollow as it was.

"Do you know *why* I didn't want you to live with your father?" Endora's floor-length swirls of purple dress lightly swished as she spun back toward the mirror. But she wasn't looking at herself. Samantha watched her mother's piercing eyes use the reflective glass as a portal to the past. Her expression softened. The lines of her expertly defined makeup muted with memories. "Devlin was the most charismatic, most handsome man I'd ever met. I fell so hard in love with him."

Endora turned back around and braced her hands behind her on the sink. "But Samantha, he's the neediest so-and-so ever born to the male race. You were such a caring child. I knew if you went with him, you'd take it upon yourself to take care of him. And you did. You sacrificed your childhood. Your dreams. It should have been the other way around."

"It wasn't that bad."

Endora tilted her eyebrows, but didn't question Sam's claim further. "Maybe not. But look at you now. You don't know what you want. You've spent so much time worrying about what Devlin wanted, then what that pin up boyfriend of yours wanted. And I'd wager Grandmother Lizabeth's ring there that you're hiding in here right now, worrying about what Dominick LaRocca wants."

Her mother couldn't have been more wrong. She was contemplating everything *she* wanted and simply couldn't have. "I'm just taking a breather." Frantically, Samantha pulled the band of gold and rubies off her finger and slapped it into her mother's hand. She didn't need the darned thing anymore. Dinner with Bomini was almost over.

Endora glanced down at the ring, then without comment, slid it into a pocket hidden in the fold of her skirt. "Dominick's a potent man. Reminds me of your father."

Endora didn't make that comparison lightly. Her intense stare only punctuated exactly what Sam had been thinking.

"Yeah, well, luckily for me, Dominick only wanted a pretend wife for the weekend. After he closes this deal with Signore Bomini, he won't need me anymore. He'll return to Chicago and run his empire. Brandon will be back and, by Monday, we'll get No Chances really up and running. I won't have time to think about how much I love that big Italian hunk."

With a melancholy nod, Endora wrapped Samantha in a gentle hug. Sam didn't fight the gesture this time, but bit her lip and willed her self-indulgent tears to remain at bay.

For the moment, she won the battle. No regrets. She'd made that promise to Nick—and to herself. But if all she had was one day left, she would make it count. And she sure as hell couldn't do that while hiding in the bathroom.

She broke away from Endora, but kept her arm wrapped around her mother's slim waist. "Come on, Mother. I'm going to introduce you to Nana Rose and Nana Fae."

"You sure you want to do that? I have a strong premonition that the three of us could cook up some delicious trouble if we're left alone too long."

Sam shook her head and laughed, her mind happily turning from her lost love with Nick to the chaos the three indomitable women could cause. Separately, they'd already done some serious damage. If not for the bounty Rose and Fae had put on Nick with the pasta label, she and Nick might never have met. And her mother's gift of oil and condoms—not to mention the ring—had paved the way for experiences of delight and of woe that still had her reeling.

What the hell. No matter how they tried, they could never conjure more grief than Sam had already worked up for herself by falling in love with a man who couldn't stay with her even if she asked.

She unlocked the bathroom door and ushered her mother through Brennan's glittering dining room to the opulent courtyard outside. The twinkling stars, the soft strains of homegrown jazz, the scents of simmering Bananas Foster, the wobbly feel of the cobblestone beneath her dainty heels—this was New Orleans. This was home.

This was what she wanted. And though she wanted Nick too, with a powerful pull she knew would ultimately tear her to shreds, she couldn't sacrifice one for the other.

She'd already forfeited her own needs in the name of love once for her father. Maybe she'd made the mistake twice, if she counted her dalliance with Anthony when she'd accompanied him on location for his films rather than grabbed a once-in-a-lifetime opportunity to start her own business. No matter how tempted she was, she couldn't allow herself to follow that same path a third time. Not if she really wanted to discover all she was.

To build a solid future, she had to stay here in New Orleans. With her family. With her new career, the first one that actually excited her to the point where she practically wanted to pinch herself and make sure this dream was real.

Luckily for her, she knew coming home to New Orleans was the most real thing she'd done. Just as she knew that her marriage to Nick was nothing more than a story they'd made up—their love affair a fantasy that couldn't withstand the intrusion of hard reality. But for tonight—this one last night— they could relish the reverie, and perhaps, make memories that would last forever.

12

AFTER SIGNING HIS NAME on the bottom line, Nick handed his ballpoint to Anita and reached across the conference table to shake Franco Bomini's aged but beefy hand. The dinner party had been a total success. After dessert, Nick invited Bomini and his grandson, the vice president of Bomini's operations, to his suite to shore up the deal. They had stayed up all night haggling details so the Italian businessman could make his scheduled flight to Rome in two hours.

Nick had been forced to leave Samantha to sleep, alone, in his bed only a few feet away, but he reasoned that the payoff would be worth the price. The deal done, Nick would have everything he wanted. Well, nearly everything. As soon as the crowd cleared out and he had Samantha to himself, he'd own the whole damn world.

Bomini scanned the pages and, satisfied, handed them over his shoulder to his grandson. *"Perfetto!* We will both make a lot of money, yes, Dominick?"

When Franco scooted his chair back, Nick rose. "That's the plan."

"I never dreamed this would all work out so well, you understand?" Bomini's broken English barely masked the depth of his emotion. The regret in the older man's gaze was impossible to miss. "My objection to you was only a means to force Rafaela to speak to me, to get past your Nana Rose, so I could apologize. I won't live forever. I had to make right what was wrong."

Nick nodded, honestly happy that the bad blood simmering between Bomini and his grandmothers had been settled, thanks to Samantha's mother, Endora. With her probing questions and some otherworldly intercession, she'd brokered peace between Bomini and Nana Fae who, it turns out, was once betrothed to the man before she met Nick's grandfather. In an act of youthful stupidity, Bomini had ended up in the bed of a well-known *pottana*, and rather than deal with the aftermath, he'd returned to the old country and left Fae behind.

His grandmother had been humiliated by his betrayal, but luckily, she'd met Salvatore Durante soon after and enjoyed a long, happy marriage. According to Endora, Salvatore himself had helped arrange the reconciliation—from the "other side." Nick preferred to believe that time simply healed all wounds.

But to Nick, time was now his greatest enemy. As soon as Bomini left his suite with a signed contract tucked in his briefcase, Samantha had no other reason to stay—except for the sensual reasons he planned to unveil, slowly and with complete detail.

"I'll expect you in Rome in, let's say, two weeks," Bomini announced as his grandson snapped his briefcase closed. "We'll have a plan for you to look over, and arrange meetings with the biggest retailers."

Nick nodded. Sounded like the way to go. The Nick he was only two days ago would have started barking orders at Anita right then and there. Setting up strategy sessions with his top staff. Brainstorming new advertising for the European market. Considering a new product or two to add to the line specifically to entice foreign buyers. But Nick couldn't think of a single thing he wanted to do *less* than work. Except for saying goodbye to Sam, which he'd soon have to do—unless he took the plunge.

By the time he responded to Bomini, he was shaking his head instead of nodding. *"Mi perdono,* Signore Bomini, but I won't be going to Rome myself."

He turned and handed his copy of the contract to Anita. "You need to memorize this, cousin." He turned back to Bomini. "Anita will handle the European distribution from this point on. She's just been promoted."

Nick held his breath, hoping Bomini wouldn't protest his selection. Bomini's Old World views were legendary and Anita was, after all, a woman—a shocked-to-silence woman at the moment. Instead, the old man smiled and grabbed Nick's cousin into a companionable hug, complete with a grandfatherly kiss on each cheek. "How lucky am I to do business with such a beautiful and intelligent *signorina?* You know, my youngest son is your age. Maybe you'd like to meet him?"

Anita smiled, but didn't say a word, causing Franco to chuckle again. After their new business associate left, Anita spun away from the door and eyed Nick warily.

"Thanks," she said finally.

Nick smiled. His announcement had indeed dazed his cousin to near speechlessness—a priceless reward if ever there was one. "You're welcome. There will be a job title change, of course. Why don't you pick it and have your business cards printed before you leave? Think you can stand jet-setting to Rome and London every few months?"

"I'll live," she quipped. "Care to clue me in on why you're suddenly handing me the deal you've been working on for as long as I can remember?"

Nick glanced at the closed bedroom door.

Anita grinned, then winced. "She left, you know."

"What?"

"Through the side door. About a half hour ago."

Nick tore into the bedroom, his heart halting at the overwhelming emptiness of the room. Her scent lingered, but her warmth was gone, sending a chill up his spine. He grabbed his jacket and wallet, scanned briefly for a note that didn't exist, then rushed back to Anita.

"Do you know where she went?"

Anita pressed her lips together. She had the crucial information he needed. Nick didn't hide his desperation or impatience, so after a long minute, she told him what he needed to know. "She said she had some cleaning up to do around her sister's house before Serena got home from her honeymoon. The plane lands at eleven-thirty."

Nick's watch read eight-thirty. He had three hours to catch Samantha. To explain. Explain what? That he loved her? That he was willing to try whatever she wanted to make a marriage work for real?

Trouble was, Nick knew exactly what Samantha wanted and needed. She hadn't said so directly, but the bits and pieces of her past that she'd revealed over the past two days added up to one clear and admirable goal—to stay in New Orleans. By doing that, she could repair the damage to her relationship with her mother and sister. See if her new venture as a bodyguard could work out permanently. And all together, restore the confidence in her own independence that had slipped whenever she'd followed a man because of love. First her father. Then that pretty-boy boyfriend.

He could give her what she needed. Space. Permanence. A foundation, like the one he'd received from his tight-knit family since the day he was born. He'd find a way. But he'd need a little help.

He nearly knocked Anita down when he rushed to kiss her for being, as always, incredibly diligent and prepared. He tore to the door, grabbed the knob, then spun back, again nearly knocking her down as she retrieved a slip of paper from her pocket.

Scribbled across the middle was the address to Serena's house.

"You're the best, Anita."

"I want a raise, Nick."

Nick laughed, but didn't reply, knowing now was not the time to negotiate a pay increase with his wonderful, smart-beyond-words cousin. In his current mood, she'd bleed him dry.

"Okay, Tab, I'm now officially homeless."

Samantha twisted the clasp on her satchel and scanned her sister's guest room for anything she might have left behind. She shooed the cat from her perch on the nightstand so she could read the clock. In a little less than an hour, her sister and her sister's new husband would be home to reclaim their house. Since she'd needed her apartment's security deposit to pay for the night-vision binoculars she'd found on the Internet, Sam had canceled her lease three weeks ago. But living at her sister's while Serena was out of the country was one thing. She wasn't about to impose on newlyweds.

With a deep breath for fortification, she marched into the kitchen, grabbed the phone and punched in the numbers to her father's cell. As expected, his assistant picked up. Also as expected, he made excuses for why Devlin couldn't take her call.

"Tell him it's a matter of life or death," she insisted, finished with being patient and understanding and doormat for her father.

"Whose life or death?"

Sam narrowed her eyes, wishing Devlin's smarmy right-hand man could see her expression. "Yours. I want to talk to my father now, understand?"

Apparently, he did. After a brief wait, Devlin's voice echoed on the other end. "Yo, baby-girl. It's about time you called to check in. How's the gumbo?"

Samantha took a second deep breath. "Expensive. I need my money, Dad."

"Sammie, the film hasn't even premiered yet. I can't start playing favorites. You aren't the only producer on this—"

She cut him off, sure she couldn't stand to argue with his expert reasoning that somehow always worked in his favor. "I'm the only producer who's your daughter."

"Honey, you know how I feel about nepotism," he said, simmering her blood with his practiced, singsong tone.

Sam bit her tongue, then remembered her first conversation with Nick about his family business and thought about all the firsthand examples she'd seen of how family members could indeed work together without ruining their relationships.

"Nepotism has nothing to do with this, Dad. You didn't hire me to do stunts because I was your daughter, you hired me because I was the best woman for the job. Then you made me a producer on the next film to avoid paying me my salary."

"But you could make so much more on your investment," he reasoned calmly.

She shook her head at the phone. If he didn't have the money, she could understand. But she knew damn well he wasn't keeping his new mistress happy with gifts from an outlet mall. The monthly mortgage payment alone on his Beverly Hills mansion was probably equal to what he owed her.

"I don't care about making more money, Dad. I didn't *choose* to put my money into this film. You chose for me. And I'm done with that. Dad, I love you, but I won't let you take advantage of me anymore. I won't allow you to use this money to keep me in your life. I worked hard. I only want what I deserve."

Silence. As more time elapsed, Sam's eyebrows rose over widening eyes. Her father was never this quiet for this long, and since she could hear him breathing, she knew they hadn't been disconnected.

"Baby-girl...Samantha, I didn't mean to take advantage of you. I just wanted to give you more."

A hot rush of moisture coated the back of her throat. "I don't want more, Dad. Not more money, anyway."

But did she want more from herself? Yeah, she wanted everything. And from Nick? She wanted so much more than he could ever, ever give.

After finalizing the amounts with her father and arranging a funds transfer, she spent the next few minutes tallying her income on a scratch pad she found in Serena's kitchen. With Nick's money, she'd already covered the outstanding rent on the No Chances office and made the last payment on the equipment she'd bought.

Now, with her hard-earned money released from her father's film, she had more than enough cash to make a new start. On her own.

She wadded the handwritten spreadsheet into a ball and shoved it in the pocket of her bag. Hefting the bulging satchel into the living room, she tried to tamp down the resentment suddenly rising inside her, anger she should feel only at herself. It was her choice to leave Nick—her choice to run away without even a goodbye.

But spending last night alone, waking up alone, was a cutting example of the life she'd lead if she tried to stay with Nick. First, she'd have to move to Chicago. And once she was there, how many lonely nights would she spend in his Lake Shore apartment while he worked out the details of some business deal or stayed late at the office to work through strategies with Anita?

Sam had a different idea altogether about what her life should be. She was done coming in second to anything or anyone, especially with people she loved.

She tossed her bag into the living room and grabbed a pillow from the couch, leaning her cheek on the brushed fabric while she thought about the cute little house she'd seen for sale last week. Situated on the very end of Bourbon Street away from the tourists and the crowds, the two-story cottage was close enough to both her sister's house and the office for her to jog to both places. A few more blocks up and she could catch the St. Charles streetcar to deliver her nearly to her mother's door in the Garden District. A place like the pink stucco town house—old and intimately small— would be just what she needed to really feel as if she'd found a home in New Orleans.

Especially when her heart was miles and miles away. In Chicago. With Nick. Who'd never even know.

She shifted on the couch, smiling ruefully when Serena's large, mixed-breed dog, Maurice, shuffled from his bed in the corner to lay his massive head on her lap. Ruffling his ears, she wondered how Nick would react when he realized she'd left without saying goodbye.

She honestly hadn't had any choice. She'd spent the entire dinner party fantasizing about getting him alone in his suite, making love with him until they were exhausted, imprinting the feel of him inside her. Instead, she'd remained awake half the night, alone, listening to the muted sounds of Nick dickering with Bomini, making his precious deal, doing what was most important to him. By the time she awoke the next morning, her dreams for a long romantic farewell had been dashed to hell. She couldn't have faced him without losing control.

Too many emotions clashed within her—anger, frustration, admiration, sorrow, grief. She'd write him a letter. Later. Maybe call. After she taught herself how to say goodbye to him, because, in all honesty, she had absolutely no idea how to form the words, much less accept the reality that she'd never see him again.

Maurice lifted his head with a growl, preluding a knock at the door. Samantha blinked, wondering how long she'd been sitting there. Were Serena and Brandon home already? Didn't they have a key? She grabbed Maurice's collar and let him drag her through the foyer.

She opened the door to find two grocery bags—with legs. Long, muscular legs encased in soft, new-looking denim.

"I have just discovered the most incredible grocery store in the nation. An A&P, right in the French Quarter, the size of my old bedroom in my mother's house back on Taylor Street. But, hey, they carry LaRocca products, so I'm sold."

Nick lowered the bags and ended his ramble as Samantha kept Maurice from attacking. Hell, while she kept herself from attacking. She'd never seen Nick dressed so casually and looking so comfortable and talking with such abandon. As if he didn't have a care in the world.

"Are you going to invite me in?"

Sam held up her hand to stop his forward motion, then shut the door in his startled face while she dragged Maurice, whimpering and barking, onto the back porch.

Nick was here? With groceries? Talking with unbridled awe about the neighborhood store where she bought her munchies?

She opened the door to find him leaning against the porch rail, a bag on each hip. His chambray shirt was unbuttoned to his breastbone, allowing her a peek at his incredibly muscular chest—the chest that had caught her eye from the label at the Food Expo—the one she now knew felt like cushioned down when cradling her cheek.

"Your Southern hospitality is slipping," he remarked, barely able to contain a grin Samantha found more and more annoying as each second ticked past.

"My sister and her husband will be home soon," she offered by way of explanation—by way of cowardly escape.

Nick's grin widened. "Actually—" he set one bag down and glanced at his watch "—they are probably just settling in for a first-rate brunch at Brennan's. I sent my limousine to pick them up at the airport. After they eat, I've instructed my driver to deliver them to your mother's house. She's organized a little welcome-home party for them. At my request, of course."

"Why?"

He blinked a few times, but his smile didn't falter. "Because I need to be alone with you."

"Why?"

He set the other bag down on the porch and took a step forward. "Because I love you."

Samantha swallowed, clutching the threshold with one hand and the knob with the other. She should slam the door in his face again. Permanently. Wasn't it bad enough that she loved him? He didn't need to add more heartbreak by admitting that the feeling was mutual.

But he'd spoken the words so softly, on such a powerful wave of emotion that his tone dipped and his volume faded, she couldn't deny the honesty he'd offered. He loved her. Okay. Fine. That didn't mean they could make a committed relationship work.

"I love you, Samantha," he repeated. "Aren't you going to say anything?"

She shook her head, but stepped back so he could

come inside. She supposed she should say something, but the obvious response caught in her throat.

Nick retrieved the bags and followed her inside, kicking the door closed behind him. "All right. I'm two for two. First, I shock Anita into near silence and then I shut you up without even trying. The two most opinionated women in the continental United States. Next to my grandmothers, that is."

Sam stifled a grin at his arrogant swagger, at the way he marched into the kitchen to deliver the groceries as if he owned the place. Leaning against the framed arch separating the living room from the kitchen, she watched him unload more food than two bags would ordinarily hold.

Andouille sausage. A full roaster chicken. Dried red beans. Two pounds of rice. A mess of vegetables, some of which she didn't recognize. A dozen or so spices. Fresh shrimp and crawfish wrapped in white paper and marked with wax crayon on the side. A long, crusty loaf of French bread, and a huge tin of LaRocca's Extra Virgin Olive Oil.

"You're planning to make me lunch?" Sam asked, knowing this conversation would be easier than addressing those three little words that had formed his heartfelt confession—the same three little words she still hadn't said to him.

"And dinner," he acknowledged, sorting the food with confident precision, his grin faltering when he found the eggs—at the bottom. He turned and sapped her breath with a sexy wink. "And breakfast, if all goes well."

"I don't think Serena and Brandon want to spend their first night home at my mother's."

"I didn't think so either, so I reserved them the finest suite at the Monteleone Hotel. You said they seemed reluctant to end their honeymoon. Your mother assured me that they'd be thrilled to have one more night."

"You can't just come in and shanghai my sister's house!"

Her vehement protest didn't slow him for a second. He perused the label of the wine he'd bought, then set it on the rack above Serena's cabinet.

"I intend to make it worth their while," he said.

She jabbed her fists onto her hips. "And what about me?"

Though she didn't mean her protest to carry a double entendre, Nick's minty-green eyes flashed with desire at the implied challenge.

"Oh, believe me..." He crossed the room in three long strides, pulling her into his arms and full against his rigid, aroused body and crackling the air with a loud, electric pop. The static charge only intensified his grin. "I intend to make it worth your while, too."

13

"AND HOW ARE YOU going to do that, Nick?" Samantha forced an impertinent stringency into her tone, forced herself to ignore her instantaneous reaction to Nick's embrace—a response that had her insides feeling like a ball of candlewax left too close to a raging fire. "Will you move to New Orleans? Settle down? Cut your business meetings short because you have a wife in purple underwear waiting for you in bed at home?"

"Sounds delicious."

She pushed herself out of his arms, creating a distance by stalking to the table, grabbing the package of seafood and tossing it into the refrigerator with a loud slam. "Don't, Nick. Don't make this some sort of fantasy. We lived the fantasy." Her voice softened. She couldn't shout about their affair. She couldn't be angry that he'd discovered all the erotic secrets she'd wanted him to find—that they'd shared one night of utter bliss. "I don't regret making love with you. But it's time to move on. It's time for *me* to move on."

Nick moved to step forward, but Samantha held him at bay with her stare—one she'd intended to be intimidating, but felt sure resembled the wide-eyed shock of a possum caught in headlights. She hadn't expected to see him again, to have this conversation.

Coward.

Wisely, Nick slid his hands into his pockets, though not very deeply, thanks to the snug fit of his jeans. She sighed.

I'm hopeless.

"It's time for me to move on, too, Samantha. That's what last night made me realize."

"Last night? Unless you count me sleeping, alone," she emphasized, "in your bed, nothing happened last night."

Nick frowned. "That's just it. Nothing happened. When Bomini was talking cost projections, I was thinking about how I wanted to touch you in the dark. When he adjusted the dates of implementation for his benefit, all I wanted to do was taste you. All of you."

He stepped closer.

She clutched the countertop behind her.

"I wasn't there when you woke up," Nick said simply. "I always want to be there when you wake up."

Samantha crossed her arms, more than aware that her stance was childlike and defensive and completely impotent to keep this man away if he chose to invade the shrinking distance between them. He'd already invaded her heart. He'd plowed straight into her soul and held her, practically powerless to deny her foolish fantasy that they might share a life beyond this weekend.

But she had to hold on to reality. The hard facts. The ugly truth.

"Imagine how you'll feel when you're in Chicago running your empire and I'm here, in New Orleans, finally taking hold of my life. Doing something I love." Samantha slid her hands onto the countertop and boosted herself up. With her feet dangling off the ground, she realized she couldn't run if Nick decided to come for her, wrap her into his arms, press her cheek to his heartbeat and force her to hear how the pounding raged just for her. Good. She couldn't run anymore. She'd have to fight. For a second time today, she had to fight for what she wanted—what she now knew she had to have. Her freedom. Her dreams.

"When I moved to L.A.," she explained, "I just wanted to be with my father. Take care of him. I was the only kid in Hollywood who *didn't* want to be in his movies. But I grew up and turned out to be really good at stunt work. Other directors requested me all the time, but I turned them down. So I could be with Devlin. So I could put him first."

Nick didn't move, but she watched his eyes soften with each word of her confession.

"Then I got hurt and couldn't work. Another director offered me the chance to consult on a film she was doing with a female lead. She wanted to use only female stuntwomen and I would have trained the other women to do what I did. Make a real name for myself. But Anthony came along. He'd just won a part in another big-budget film, and I put aside my dream again. Went with him halfway across the world to sit in his dressing room and wait." She closed her eyes, marveling at how she could finally admit all this to Nick, to herself, at the moment when she least wanted to talk about her past. But she owed Nick the truth. She owed him an honest goodbye.

"I'm not your father, Samantha. And I'm sure as hell not Anthony Marks."

She shook her head, denying that she'd meant to make any comparison between them. Nick wasn't the reason she couldn't leave. Not really. *She* was the reason.

"All my life, I've followed the men I loved at the expense of my needs. My dreams. I do love you, Nick, but loving you makes me want to do it again. I can't. I'm not that same girl anymore. Before you came, before we met, I was just starting to see that I have to put myself first. If we'd met two months ago..."

"We probably wouldn't have fallen in love. I love the woman you are now, Sam. The woman who has to put herself first."

"But I can't go with you, Nick. Please don't ask me to."

"I won't." He stepped nearer then, his hands clasped just in front of him, as if he fought the urge to grab her, shake her, coax her to change her mind. "I wouldn't."

Though she heard the answer she wanted, her heart still cracked within her chest, allowing a hot stream of sorrow to burn into her belly, then up the back of her throat, until it welled up in her eyes.

She pulled in a ragged breath, forcing her words out on a shaky exhalation. "Then there's nothing left to say."

"There's always the part where I tell you that I'm moving to New Orleans."

Her eyes flashed wide. "What?"

He struggled to contain that wonderful, delicious, arrogant grin that made her insides clench with need each and every time. "I haven't worked out the details, but I put Anita on the European distribution. Now I'm thinking about expanding the LaRocca product line, working in other ethnic foods like authentic Creole and Cajun stuff. Maybe enticing this Miss Lily you and your mother keep bragging about to sell us some recipes."

Sam pressed her palm to her chest, certain Nick could see the leap her heart made at the possibility that he was telling her the truth.

"What about your family?"

Nick shrugged. "That's what e-mail and airplanes are for. Chicago is only a two-hour flight away." With that declaration, he dismissed the topic and looked around her sister's kitchen with narrowed, assessing eyes. "We'll need a place with a bigger kitchen. All state-of-the-art. I saw a building a few blocks from here that was zoned for business. I called the listing agent and we're meeting tomorrow. Any preferences on where we might live?"

Sam shook her head, not because she didn't know— she did—but because she was trying to dislodge the fog clouding her brain, marring her ability to think.

"There's this cottage on Bourbon Street..."

Nick's grin nearly split his face in two and for the first time since she'd known him, he laughed. Not a chuckle or a snicker, but an explosive burst from his belly—unguarded, unchecked and totally unrefined. With a wild swoop, he lifted her off the counter and swung her around, making her dizzy with happiness. When he lowered her ever so slowly to the ground, ensuring that every inch of her body slid down every inch of his, the light-headedness turned to irrepressible desire.

He crooked his finger beneath her chin. "I never thought I'd ever fall in love, Samantha. With you, it took less than two days."

She smiled, lifting herself on tiptoe to place a soft kiss on his chin. "Imagine what we could do with the rest of our lives."

Nick swept a trail of kisses across her temple and down her cheek. "We won't have to imagine. But first..." Again he looked around the kitchen, and again, Serena's neat and tidy space wasn't up to par. He released her and looked out the window over the sink, satisfied at what he saw outside.

Until Maurice jumped up from the other side and greeted him with a growling snap.

"Is there somewhere else you can put that dog?"

Samantha grabbed a box of dog biscuits from the cabinet, then enticed Maurice into the guest room, where she dragged his bed and water dish. When she returned to the kitchen, Nick was gone. Judging by the back door, which he'd propped open with a chair, Nick had ventured onto the porch.

She slipped outside, thrilled, excited, giddy with desire and happiness and love. Nick had found a way to follow *her*, to create an entire new business so they could be together. He valued her needs enough to alter his own.

All for her.

The hundred-year-old wood on Serena's back porch creaked beneath Sam's weight, the rubbery squeal echoing in the quiet, walled-in space behind the house. Like most French Quarter residents, Serena had created a wild, intricate garden behind her house, overrun with ivy that climbed up the ten-foot brick walls and dripping with fern and jasmine and big, leafy plants Sam couldn't name. A small, trickling fountain bubbled in the center, providing sweet music for the natural silence. Sunlight struggled in vain to touch the shadows, and Sam was glad. Especially when she stepped off the porch and caught sight of Nick watching her from the base of the stone sculpture that centered the fountain.

When she crossed the stepping stones to meet him, he glanced over his shoulder at the statue, a Grecian couple, naked and entwined. "Your sister has interesting taste."

Sam swallowed a grin. "You should see the fountain at her spa. Most erotic thing you've ever seen."

Nick's smile faded, and heat, male and needful, burned from his eyes. "You're the most erotic thing I've ever seen."

She looked down at her clothing, smoothing her hands from her midriff, bared by her cutoff T-shirt, to the waistband of her soft, floppy knit pants. Her hair was snared in a loose ponytail, which she immediately released. She'd spent the morning cleaning and packing, giving no attention to her appearance.

Yet, reflected in Nick's eyes, she was the most beautiful woman in the world.

"I probably look better in the purple underwear."

Nick's body instantly reacted. A rush of hot need throbbed to his groin, then bolted straight to his brain to flash images and sensations of Samantha rescuing him, Samantha touching him, Samantha opening her body and soul for him to explore. Just two nights ago, he'd learned about giving and sharing the parts of himself he'd buried, protected, denied.

Never again. Not if Samantha accepted the proposal that, despite his overwhelming desire for her, still lodged in the back of his throat.

"You think? I barely remember the purple underwear. Maybe later, you can remind me. Right now, I have a standard to live up to."

Sam gasped when Nick dropped to his knee and produced her great-grandmother's ruby ring from his pocket. She'd returned it to her mother last night, but before they left the restaurant, Endora had given it back to him. She made him promise to put the ring to good use, muttering something about destiny and spiritual ownership.

Despite his inability to believe in such nonsense, he'd carried the ring with him ever since, tucked in his breast pocket during the meeting with Bomini, and slipped into his jeans pocket during his shopping spree this morning. He'd known he had to give it back to Samantha, but he wouldn't unless he did so the right way.

"Where did you—"

He cut off her question by shaking his head. "Your mother claims the ring's aura is interwoven with mine."

She bit her lip. "I hate to admit this, but my mother's hardly ever wrong."

"Then if I ask you to marry me," he whispered, taking her left hand and slipping the ruby onto her finger to the sound of her sigh, "to be my wife and lover and keeper of my soul, you'll say yes?"

She looked at the ring, examining it on her hand as if she'd never seen the glittering gem before. He watched her eyes glisten, marveling at how the nearly imperceptible increase of shine in her eyes clutched at the recesses of his heart. God, he loved this woman.

She tugged him up to stand, then curled into his arms. He breathed in her scent, spread his hands around her bare middle and stamped her warm body with his needful touch.

"Yes, Nick. I'll be all those things for you. With you."

Nick kissed her, hungry for the taste of her, starving for the spice her simple presence added to his life, to his soul. He could kiss her forever, touch her forever. She was a craving he'd never, ever satisfy—though he intended to enjoy trying.

"But you'll have to promise me one thing," she added once they broke to gasp for some air.

He held her back a few inches, loath to release her, but intrigued by the mischievous lilt in her voice. "What's that?"

With her signature quick reflexes, she twisted out of his embrace and whipped her T-shirt over her head in one smooth and graceful move. His eyes drank in the sight of her, free and aroused and wearing a satin bra cut sinfully to cup her breast, but not cover them.

This bra was red.

His mouth watered and his jeans tightened. With measured slowness, she slid her pants down, over her hips, revealing first her thighs, then knees, calves, ankles. She stepped back to him, leaving her clothing behind, her fingers skimming the triangular top of the equally scarlet panties.

"Seems I inherited a complete collection of naughty underthings recently." She whispered the news as her lips nibbled from the center of his chest, up his neck, to his chin.

He swallowed, watching her nipples brush the material of his shirt while she worked each of his buttons. He managed a casual, "Really?" just before she placed an opened-mouth kiss on the center of his now-bare chest.

"Mmm-hmm."

She swiped a stiff-tongued lick across his nipple, flaming his desire so that he nearly shook trying to remain still.

She popped the top button of his jeans, then slid his zipper in one fluid move, the rasp of the metal accompanying his sharp intake of breath.

"Until my experience in the purple ones, with you, I never knew how sexy they could make a woman feel. How decadent. How insatiable." Her hands dipped into his waistband and clutched at his buttocks with an intense squeeze.

"Uh-huh," he muttered, noting that somewhere beyond the haze of his need, he was supposed to be agreeing to something she wanted. He blinked, trying to follow her hints, but gave up the minute she dragged his jeans down his legs.

"I'm feeling pretty darned ravenous right now, Nick. Promise you'll do something to satisfy me?"

That invitation he could follow. He kicked his jeans into the undergrowth and lifted Samantha into his arms, eyeing a bench two or three strides away.

Triangles of cool tile bit through his cotton boxers

when he sat, but the feel of Samantha wrapping her legs around his waist instantly fired a steady, throbbing heat.

"Satisfying hunger is what I do best, sweetheart. You're going to be the most satiated woman in New Orleans, sexy underthings or no sexy underthings, for the rest of your life."

She licked her lips.

Then licked his.

And the only thing she could think to say was, "Mmm, mmm, good."

*Three sizzling love stories
by today's hottest writers
can be found in...*

Midnight Fantasies....

Feel the heat!

Available July 2001

MYSTERY LOVER—Vicki Lewis Thompson

When an unexpected storm hits, rancher Jonas Garfield
takes cover in a nearby cave...and finds himself seduced
senseless by an enigmatic temptress who refuses to tell him
her name. All he knows is that this sexy woman wants him.
And for Jonas, that's enough—for now....

AFTER HOURS—Stephanie Bond

Michael Pierce has always considered costume shop
owner Rebecca Valentine no more than an associate—
until he drops by her shop one night and witnesses the
mousy wallflower's transformation into a seductive siren.
Suddenly he's desperate to know her much better.
But which woman is the real Rebecca?

SHOW AND TELL—Kimberly Raye

A naughty lingerie party. A forbidden fantasy. When Texas
bad boy Dallas Jericho finds a slip of paper left over from
the party, he is surprised—and aroused—to discover that he
is good girl Laney Merriweather's wildest fantasy. So what
can he do but show the lady what she's been missing....

Visit us at www.eHarlequin.com   PHMIDNIGHTR

If you enjoyed what you just read,
then we've got an offer you can't resist!

Take 2 bestselling
love stories FREE!
Plus get a FREE surprise gift!

Clip this page and mail it to Harlequin Reader Service®

IN U.S.A.	IN CANADA
3010 Walden Ave.	P.O. Box 609
P.O. Box 1867	Fort Erie, Ontario
Buffalo, N.Y. 14240-1867	L2A 5X3

YES! Please send me 2 free Harlequin Temptation® novels and my free surprise gift. Then send me 4 brand-new novels every month, which I will receive before they're available in stores. In the U.S.A., bill me at the bargain price of $3.34 plus 25¢ delivery per book and applicable sales tax, if any*. In Canada, bill me at the bargain price of $3.80 plus 25¢ delivery per book and applicable taxes**. That's the complete price and a savings of 10% off the cover prices—what a great deal! I understand that accepting the 2 free books and gift places me under no obligation ever to buy any books. I can always return a shipment and cancel at any time. Even if I never buy another book from Harlequin, the 2 free books and gift are mine to keep forever. So why not take us up on our invitation. You'll be glad you did!

142 HEN C22U
342 HEN C22V

Name	(PLEASE PRINT)	
Address	Apt.#	
City	State/Prov.	Zip/Postal Code

* Terms and prices subject to change without notice. Sales tax applicable in N.Y.
** Canadian residents will be charged applicable provincial taxes and GST.
 All orders subject to approval. Offer limited to one per household.
® are registered trademarks of Harlequin Enterprises Limited.

TEMP00   ©1998 Harlequin Enterprises Limited

*Harlequin truly does
make any time special....
This year we are celebrating
weddings in style!*

A Walk Down the Aisle
WEDDING CELEBRATION

To help us celebrate, we want you to tell us how wearing the
Harlequin wedding gown will make your wedding day special. As
the grand prize, Harlequin will offer one lucky bride the chance to
"Walk Down the Aisle" in the Harlequin wedding gown!

There's more...

For her honeymoon, she and her groom will spend five nights at the
Hyatt Regency Maui. As part of this five-night honeymoon at the
hotel renowned for its romantic attractions, the couple will enjoy a candlelit
dinner for two in Swan Court, a sunset sail on the hotel's catamaran, and
duet spa treatments.

A HYATT RESORT AND SPA   Maui • Molokai • Lanai

To enter, please write, in, 250 words or less, how wearing the Harlequin
wedding gown will make your wedding day special. The entry will be
judged based on its emotionally compelling nature, its originality and
creativity, and its sincerity. This contest is open to Canadian and U.S.
residents only and to those who are 18 years of age and older. There is no
purchase necessary to enter. Void where prohibited. See further contest
rules attached. Please send your entry to:

Walk Down the Aisle Contest

In Canada	In U.S.A.
P.O. Box 637	P.O. Box 9076
Fort Erie, Ontario	3010 Walden Ave.
L2A 5X3	Buffalo, NY 14269-9076

You can also enter by visiting www.eHarlequin.com
Win the Harlequin wedding gown and the vacation of a lifetime!
The deadline for entries is October 1, 2001.

HARLEQUIN®
Makes any time special ®

PHWDACONT

HARLEQUIN WALK DOWN THE AISLE TO MAUI CONTEST 1197
OFFICIAL RULES
NO PURCHASE NECESSARY TO ENTER

1. To enter, follow directions published in the offer to which you are responding. Contest begins April 2, 2001, and ends on October 1, 2001. Method of entry may vary. Mailed entries must be postmarked by October 1, 2001, and received by October 8, 2001.

2. Contest entry may be, at times, presented via the Internet, but will be restricted solely to residents of certain geographic areas that are disclosed on the Web site. To enter via the Internet, if permissible, access the Harlequin Web site (www.eHarlequin.com) and follow the directions displayed online. Online entries must be received by 11:59 p.m. E.S.T. on October 1, 2001.

   In lieu of submitting an entry online, enter by mail by hand-printing (or typing) on an 8½" x 11" plain piece of paper, your name, address (including zip code), Contest number/name and in 250 words or fewer, why winning a Harlequin wedding dress would make your wedding day special. Mail via first-class mail to: Harlequin Walk Down the Aisle Contest 1197, (in the U.S.) P.O. Box 9076, 3010 Walden Avenue, Buffalo, NY 14269-9076, (in Canada) P.O. Box 637, Fort Erie, Ontario L2A 5X3, Canada.

   Limit one entry per person, household address and e-mail address. Online and/or mailed entries received from persons residing in geographic areas in which Internet entry is not permissible will be disqualified.

3. Contests will be judged by a panel of members of the Harlequin editorial, marketing and public relations staff based on the following criteria:

   * Originality and Creativity—50%
   * Emotionally Compelling—25%
   * Sincerity—25%

   In the event of a tie, duplicate prizes will be awarded. Decisions of the judges are final.

4. All entries become the property of Torstar Corp. and will not be returned. No responsibility is assumed for lost, late, illegible, incomplete, inaccurate, nondelivered or misdirected mail or misdirected e-mail, for technical, hardware or software failures of any kind, lost or unavailable network connections, or failed, incomplete, garbled or delayed computer transmission or any human error which may occur in the receipt or processing of the entries in this Contest.

5. Contest open only to residents of the U.S. (except Puerto Rico) and Canada, who are 18 years of age or older, and is void wherever prohibited by law; all applicable laws and regulations apply. Any litigation within the Province of Quebec respecting the conduct or organization of a publicity contest may be submitted to the Régie des alcools, des courses et des jeux for a ruling. Any litigation respecting the awarding of a prize may be submitted to the Régie des alcools, des courses et des jeux only for the purpose of helping the parties reach a settlement. Employees and immediate family members of Torstar Corp. and D. L. Blair, Inc., their affiliates, subsidiaries and all other agencies, entities and persons connected with the use, marketing or conduct of this Contest are not eligible to enter. Taxes on prizes are the sole responsibility of winners. Acceptance of any prize offered constitutes permission to use winner's name, photograph or other likeness for the purposes of advertising, trade and promotion on behalf of Torstar Corp., its affiliates and subsidiaries without further compensation to the winner, unless prohibited by law.

6. Winners will be determined no later than November 15, 2001, and will be notified by mail. Winners will be required to sign and return an Affidavit of Eligibility form within 15 days after winner notification. Noncompliance within that time period may result in disqualification and an alternative winner may be selected. Winners of trip must execute a Release of Liability prior to ticketing and must possess required travel documents (e.g. passport, photo ID) where applicable. Trip must be completed by November 2002. No substitution of prize permitted by winner. Torstar Corp. and D. L. Blair, Inc., their parents, affiliates, and subsidiaries are not responsible for errors in printing or electronic presentation of Contest, entries and/or game pieces. In the event of printing or other errors which may result in unintended prize values or duplication of prizes, all affected game pieces or entries shall be null and void. If for any reason the Internet portion of the Contest is not capable of running as planned, including infection by computer virus, bugs, tampering, unauthorized intervention, fraud, technical failures, or any other causes beyond the control of Torstar Corp. which corrupt or affect the administration, secrecy, fairness, integrity or proper conduct of the Contest, Torstar Corp. reserves the right, at its sole discretion, to disqualify any individual who tampers with the entry process and to cancel, terminate, modify or suspend the Contest or the Internet portion thereof. In the event of a dispute regarding an online entry, the entry will be deemed submitted by the authorized holder of the e-mail account submitted at the time of entry. Authorized account holder is defined as the natural person who is assigned to an e-mail address by an Internet access provider, online service provider or other organization that is responsible for arranging e-mail address for the domain associated with the submitted e-mail address. **Purchase or acceptance of a product offer does not improve your chances of winning.**

7. Prizes: (1) Grand Prize—A Harlequin wedding dress (approximate retail value: $3,500) and a 5-night/6-day honeymoon trip to Maui, HI, including round-trip air transportation provided by Maui Visitors Bureau from Los Angeles International Airport (winner is responsible for transportation to and from Los Angeles International Airport) and a Harlequin Romance Package, including hotel accomodations (double occupancy) at the Hyatt Regency Maui Resort and Spa, dinner for (2) two at Swan Court, a sunset sail on Kiele V and a spa treatment for the winner (approximate retail value: $4,000); (5) Five runner-up prizes of a $1000 gift certificate to selected retail outlets to be determined by Sponsor (retail value $1000 ea.). Prizes consist of only those items listed as part of the prize. Limit one prize per winner. All prizes are valued in U.S. currency.

   For a list of winners (available after December 17, 2001) send a self-addressed, stamped envelope to: Harlequin Walk Down the Aisle Contest 1197 Winners, P.O. Box 4200 Blair, NE 68009-4200 or you may access the www.eHarlequin.com Web site through January 15, 2002.

Contest sponsored by Torstar Corp., P.O. Box 9042, Buffalo, NY 14269-9042, U.S.A.

PHWDACONT2

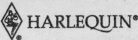
HARLEQUIN®

makes any time special—online...

eHARLEQUIN.com

your romantic escapes

•—Indulgences—

♥ Monthly guides to indulging yourself, such as:
  ★ Tub Time: A guide for bathing beauties
  ★ Magic Massages: A treat for tired feet

•—Horoscopes—

♥ Find your daily Passionscope, weekly Lovescopes and Erotiscopes

♥ Try our compatibility game

•—Reel Love—

♥ Read all the latest romantic movie reviews

•—Royal Romance—

♥ Get the latest scoop on your favorite royal romances

•—Romantic Travel—

♥ For the most romantic destinations, hotels and travel activities

All this and more available at
www.eHarlequin.com
on Women.com Networks

HINTE1R